MW01534818

SILVIA VIOLET
Unexpected
ENGAGEMENT

Unexpected Engagement

Simon McLeod was a promising young naval captain before his ship was attacked and CIA agents forced him to fake his death and join their ranks. Since that horrible night, Simon has focused on finding the men responsible for ending his career. He's close now, but he needs help from the man he loves. The problem is Edgar is straight, has no idea how Simon feels, and threatened to strangle him the last time they were together.

After years of using his medical expertise to patch Simon up after ill-advised missions, Edgar told Simon not to come running to him anymore. Watching Simon self-destruct was too painful. But when Simon shows up on Edgar's doorstep covered in blood, Edgar can't turn him away. He also can't fight the feelings he has for Simon, feelings that go way beyond friendship.

Neither man thought he'd ever truly be happy again, but if they can survive a final dangerous mission, they might be able to prove themselves wrong.

Silvia Violet

Unexpected Engagement by Silvia Violet

Copyright © 2015 by Silvia Violet

Cover art by Meredith Russell

Edited by Erika Orrick

All Rights Reserved. No part of this eBook may be used or reproduced in any manner whatsoever without written permission except in brief quotations embodied in critical articles or reviews.

Published in the United States of America.

Unexpected Engagement is a work of fiction. Names, places, characters, and incidents are either the product of the author's imagination or are fictionalized. Any resemblance to any actual persons, living or dead, is entirely coincidental.

PROLOGUE

Five Years Ago

Simon fought to hide his disgust as he stood, flanked by his top officers, watching a man in an expensive pinstripe suit emerge from the helo. A fucking gorgeous man. From the way his movements were calculated to draw attention, Simon was sure he knew how good he looked. Eye candy or not, Simon didn't have time for this shit. He was less than a year into his first command and he needed to attend to the demands of his ship, not schmooze Daniel Radzwill, fucking civilian weapons contractor.

Why the hell he'd insisted on visiting Simon's ship was a mystery. There were plenty of vessels far more important for him to tour in far less dangerous waters with captains whose records would impress Mr. Radzwill far more than his. Since the last-minute visit had been arranged the day before, something had been niggling at the back of Simon's mind. His instincts said something was off, but what could it be?

"Welcome aboard the *Ridgeway*, Mr. Radzwill," Simon said, offering his hand.

Radzwill took Simon's hand and gave a firm shake, his touch lingering just a second too long. *Insolent bastard.* If Radzwill thought sex came with the tour of Simon's ship, he was way off base.

4

"Thank you, Captain. I appreciate your agreeing to host me on short notice."

As if he had a choice. "I've arranged for you to start with a tour if that meets with your approval."

Radzwill slowly looked Simon up and down. "So far *everything* meets with my approval."

Could he be any more blatant?

"I'd like a meeting with you, Captain, a private one," Radzwill purred.

There had to be an ulterior motive to this flirtation. What the hell did he think Simon could do for him? Simon might be the youngest captain in seventy years, but he still didn't have the power to decide on the Navy's weapons contractors. "That may be impossible today. I—"

"It is imperative that I speak with you." Something in his tone made Simon uneasy and not because he feared how far across the line Radzwill would step—he was more than capable of fending off a rich boy's grabby hands. What bothered Simon was that the easy insolence Radzwill had spoken with earlier had disappeared. He looked serious and… worried? Something was definitely off, and the best way to figure it out was to have the requested meeting.

"I'll make the time, then, immediately after your tour."

When Mr. Radzwill entered the captain's office where Simon awaited him, he set a flash drive down on the table between them. "You need to see the contents of this drive."

Simon studied the man, then picked up the drive and turned it over in his hand. "You're not a weapons dealer, are you, Mr. Radzwill?"

The man shook his head. "No, I'm not. And call me Danny, it's more or less my real name."

"What the hell are you doing here?"

"Hopefully saving a lot of lives."

"Who sent you?" Simon thought he knew. There'd been chatter about a CIA operation that involved his fleet.

"That's not important."

"It is if you want me to listen."

Danny rolled his eyes. "Fine. I'm with the CIA. I always feel like a douche in a bad movie saying that. Now look at what's on the drive. I'll wait as long as I need to."

Danny still had the flirtatious lilt to his voice, but something in his eyes was deadly serious. Simon had already anticipated a long day before he'd been told to ready the ship for a visitor. But this... He kept hoping it was all a bad dream and he'd wake up with nothing more than a few incompetent men and a fuckload of paperwork to bitch about.

Simon opened his laptop and began skimming the files on the drive. After reading through a few documents, Simon felt so sick he wasn't sure he could speak. This couldn't be happening. He wasn't naïve. He knew there were bad seeds in the Navy like anywhere else. There were officers who made payoffs, bargained with enemies, took bribes to not see illegal activity. But this was so much more. The information on this drive implied that several high-ranking officers, as well as contacts at the FBI and in Congress, were facilitating attacks on the US military in exchange for money. He looked away, not wanting

playing him? The CIA had tried to recruit him out of the Academy, but he'd never trusted the shadowy bastards.

Nine months. That's all he'd had of this command and it had gone so fucking well. He'd been right where he wanted to be. "You damn well better know what you're talking about."

"I'm telling you the truth," Danny said. "I can't have anyone else verify what I'm telling you because I can't reveal the identity of anyone I'm working with. We're all shadows, and I'm here to drag you into the darkness. I hate it, especially when you're the golden boy—all sunshine and light and ease of command—but it's my job and I'm just as good at it as you are at yours."

"Corrupting people is your job?"

Danny sighed. "I think of it more as turning out the lights."

"Fucking fuck!" Simon slammed his hand down on his desk, making the laptop slide across the surface.

Danny smiled as he steadied it. "I couldn't have said it better."

"How do we stop them?"

"Together. There's an operative who's been on the ship since you sailed. I'll send him back in my place."

"So someone's been spying on me?"

"Not you so much as your crew, but yes."

Simon wanted to slap Danny's smug smile off his face. "Son of a bitch."

"He can be. Generally, he's rather a nice man, much nicer than me, but he's deadly when he needs to be. I'm more experienced, though, so he goes and I stay."

"How? In disguise, or does he look like you?" Simon considered his crew, but he knew there was no one who looked like Danny. He wouldn't have forgotten such a man.

"He can come close enough in the dark when people are expecting to see me. He'll leave tonight. And then I'll be here, but only as a shadow."

"So you'll do what? Hide in my closet?"

"Something like that." Danny smiled and Simon did too, though it pissed him off that Danny could charm him. None of what Simon had just learned felt real yet, and it wouldn't until the order actually came.

"Tomorrow you're scheduled to dock. You'll give your crew shore leave, as many of them as you possibly can. Then when the order comes, we sail."

Simon nodded.

That was the moment Simon's life went to hell. When his ship was attacked, he succeeded in saving most of his crew, and Edgar, the man who'd become Simon's best friend, saved Simon. Danny disappeared for months after the incident. When he resurfaced, he helped Simon transform into something he never thought he'd be: a spy. He was no longer a captain, no longer happy in the light giving orders and receiving acclamations. He'd become a creature who slid through shadows and seduced people to their deaths.

CHAPTER ONE

Present Day

Keep moving. Just keep moving.

Simon winced as the wound in his side twinged. There was a bullet lodged there. He wasn't sure exactly how bad off he was, and he couldn't afford to stop and examine it. The last thing he needed to do was draw attention to himself. If he could find a car and get out of there, he could probably survive long enough to find help.

His cover was blown, so there was no way he could go to an ER. There weren't any safe houses nearby, and they didn't come equipped with doctors anyway. The wound was beyond something he could deal with on his own. The bullet must not have hit anything vital because he wasn't dead yet, but it had been in him for almost twenty-four hours.

"Fuckin' charmed ye are," Danny would've said if he'd been there, but Danny was too far away to help him, and Simon wouldn't risk him anyway. He'd sent Danny a single message after he'd outdistanced his captors, telling him things had gone to shit. Then he'd tossed his phone and kept moving. When had he last slept? He wasn't sure. Two days ago maybe. He hadn't eaten either, but what he really needed was water. He'd have to steal some soon.

He turned into a parking lot, forcing himself to stay upright and not favor his side. No one would remember him if he could just look like a normal guy. If he was limping or they saw the blood soaking his T-shirt—thank God it was cold and the leather coat he'd stolen from one of his captors covered the bloodstains—he was screwed.

He walked across the parking lot as if he knew where he was going, scanning the cars for a good prospect. The street in front of him wavered.

Come on. Don't pass out now.

Finally, he found a car that suited him, an older nondescript sedan, one of the most common models on the road. He had it started in a matter of seconds.

Where do I go now?

Edgar. His subconscious had been whispering the name, tantalizing him with it.

He'd sworn he wouldn't call Edgar again. Edgar was sick of picking up the pieces after Simon took insane risks. Would Edgar deem this mission insane? Simon supposed most people would think so, especially since he'd known he was being set up going in. But he was closing in on the organization who'd attacked the *Ridgeway*. Finally, after five years. Surely Edgar would understand if Simon needed him just one more time.

Simon put the car in gear and backed out of the parking space. He spared a second's regret that the car's owner would wind up stranded—he wasn't quite the cold bastard Edgar thought he was. But this was a matter of life and death, not just his own. The intel he'd gotten before he'd been made could save untold numbers of people. He needed to live long enough to pass it on.

Simon didn't know his exact location, but he was somewhere outside of Norfolk. Edgar's apartment in Richmond was at least an hour and a half away. Could Simon stay conscious that long? He hoped to God so, and he had a key if Edgar wasn't home. He still hadn't gotten any water, but he didn't want to stop for it. All he wanted was Edgar.

***

"No! I'm not leaving you," Edgar shouted.

Simon pushed weakly at Edgar's shoulder. "Get off this ship. That is an order."

"You're bleeding all over the deck. I've got to stop it."

"I'd rather bleed out than drown. Go!"

"No." Edgar wouldn't leave Simon to die, he'd sacrificed enough.

"There's no saving me, but you can save yourself." Simon drew in a rattly breath. "Edgar, please."

Simon had grown even paler. Edgar hadn't thought that was possible.

"Please," Simon gasped, eyes wide. "Go." His eyes fluttered closed and his head dropped back.

Edgar searched desperately for a pulse. "No!" A wave crashed over the side as the ship listed farther to port. Edgar threw his arm up as if he could hold back the sea. When he opened his eyes, Simon was gone, washed overboard. "Noooo! I could've saved him. Noooo!"

Edgar bolted upright, chest heaving as he gasped for breath. He wasn't on the *Ridgeway*. Simon was alive. At least as far as he knew, not that he had any clue where the bastard was. It had been weeks since he'd had a text from Simon. They used to communicate daily when Simon wasn't on an assignment, but that had ended after he'd sent Simon packing, saying he couldn't keep patching him up so he could try to get himself killed again. But Simon hadn't cut off all communication. He still sent a text about once a week, even if they were mostly impersonal updates. The length of this current silence was starting to worry Edgar, and the nightmares were getting worse.

Edgar rubbed at his temples. His ears rang as if the explosions going off in his dream had been real. His mind tried to suck him right back into the horror even though he was no longer sleeping. That bastard Simon had actually thought Edgar would leave him there when he was critically wounded. Somehow, Simon had known what was coming, but he hadn't bothered to share it with Edgar or any of the other senior officers on the ship. Typical. Simon decided to save the day on his own. Or maybe not completely on his own; Danny had been there. Edgar just hadn't met that seductive little shit at that point. But Edgar would never leave his captain, his friend, the man he... No, that thought was best shoved back into his subconscious where it belonged.

Edgar threw back the covers and forced himself out of bed. Dreams of the attack on the *Ridgeway* and the other horrors he'd experienced in the years had been an occasional problem, but since his breakup with Simon—*what the fuck? Why am I calling it a breakup? We weren't dating*—they'd been coming more and more frequently. Now they were a nightly event. In his dreams, Simon was always taken from him by something beyond his control—monsters, monstrous forms made of fire, or whirlwinds that had a life of their own. Something always tore Simon from him before Edgar could heal him.

You miss him.

No. Yes. But I can't keep rescuing him when he doesn't truly want to be saved.

If he didn't want you to save him, he wouldn't keep calling you.

He only calls me to bail him out. He chooses to risk his life again and again, taking missions that put him in situations no sane person would agree to.

Edgar banged his hand against the doorframe, making it rattle. He'd tear it apart and the whole bathroom with it if the destruction would really take his anger away, but nothing short of Simon acting like he still valued his life would do that.

Edgar stumbled toward the kitchen, where he poured a glass of bourbon and downed it in one go. After he set the glass in the sink, he glanced at the clock. Two AM. No wonder he still felt so tired. He'd only been asleep for an hour and a half. He glanced toward his bedroom. He needed sleep, but he was sure the dream would follow him if he went back to bed. Instead, he pulled a blanket out of the hall closet and settled on the couch. He'd been sleeping there more and more frequently. His bed felt too lonely, not that there'd ever been anyone in it regularly.

There's one person you wish were there.

No, that would be an utter disaster.

Would it really?

***

Edgar rubbed his eyes and turned over, which nearly resulted in him falling off the bed. What the fuck? Oh right, he wasn't on the bed. He was on the couch. Again. He checked the clock. Four AM. He'd guessed right. Nowhere near time to get up. So what the hell had woken him this time?

He listened, waiting for a clue.

A few seconds later, he heard it. A whisper of sound just outside the door of his apartment. Most people wouldn't notice, but he'd honed his instincts in the years he spent as a medic for a SEAL team, long before he was assigned to the *Ridgeway* and Simon. Sometimes hearing a whisper of sound meant you lived to see another day.

He moved silently as he crossed the room and unlocked the drawer where he kept his gun. It had been a while since serious trouble had come to find him, but he wasn't taking any chances.

He approached the door, heart pounding, ready to defend himself any way he could. The lock began to move. The fucker was going to come in. Edgar took cover behind a sturdy chair.

The knob turned. Seconds passed. Then the door swung open.

Edgar aimed for the intruder, finger on the trigger.

"Edgar, it's me." Simon pushed the door closed behind him and Edgar lowered his gun, flicking on the safety.

"Simon, what the fuck? Have you ever heard of knocking? I could have shot you."

"Someone beat you to it. And why knock when I have a key." Simon pulled his coat away to reveal a dark stain on his side.

"What happened?" Edgar hated the way his stomach knotted as memories rushed to his mind: Simon bleeding all over the deck. His blood staining the floor in the prison where they were taken after being "rescued" from the *Ridgeway*. Simon lying on that cold concrete floor. Simon flatlining while Edgar fought to save him.

"Someone shot me. I thought you got that already." Ah, Simon, ever the comedian.

"Why?" Edgar knew he should do something to help, but he was frozen in place. This was exactly why he'd quit going on missions with Simon after the disaster in South America. Edgar was no good in a crisis anymore.

Simon shrugged. "I tend to give people a lot of reasons."

"No shit."

Finally remembering how to move, Edgar wrapped an arm around Simon and led him to the couch.

"You could have called, let me know you were coming."

"I had to get rid of my phone. I tried to think of somewhere else. But there wasn't anyone close enough." His words were stilted. Edgar fought not to think of the night Simon had died and been revived.

"How long have you been on the run?"

Simon shrugged and then winced. "I don't know. What day is it?"

"Fuck, Simon. When were you shot?"

Simon closed his eyes and tipped his head back on the couch. "Yesterday morning."

"And you've—" Edgar cut himself off. There was no point in arguing with Simon. There never had been.

He grabbed some medical supplies and came back. "You couldn't call in, get someone to help you?"

"You'll help me." Simon's soft smile would win him anything, and he fucking knew it. Edgar wasn't going to refuse him when he showed up wounded. He was a doctor, for fuck's sake.

"Yeah, I will." *Despite telling you to fuck off and not come to me for help again.* "But I know you have other resources."

Simon shook his head. "Not on this one."

"Danny?"

"Got a message to him, but he's… not in a position to help."

Edgar knew there was a story there, but he wasn't going to push, not now.

"And the ER?" Edgar knew that was a pointless suggestion as soon as he said it. Simon would never risk his cover in an ER.

Simon shook his head. "No hospitals."

"Of course not."

"These guys are good. I couldn't risk them following me to a hospital."

"So you thought you'd lead them to me?" Edgar asked, but the words came out sad rather than bitter. He wasn't going to stay mad at Simon. He'd never been able to.

Simon frowned. "I lost them. I really think I did. But you can defend yourself."

"Yeah, yeah, just let me look at you." Edgar

knew Simon was right and yet he was so fucking tired of this, tired of being the place Simon only came when he was desperate.

CHAPTER TWO

Simon hated the condemnation in Edgar's eyes. He'd tried to think of anywhere else he dared to go for help, but he didn't trust many people now. Danny was out. Jackson was hours away. Simon would never survive that trip, and even if he did, Jackson would kill him for putting Addy in danger. Addy was stronger than Jackson gave him credit for, but he was a civilian and always had been. He had nerve and determination but no training. He wouldn't last against the enemies Simon had made.

Danny had tried to join Simon on the mission, but Danny had Sport now, and they were so goddamn happy together. Simon had refused to let Danny risk himself. So now, left on his own, Simon had run to the one place he'd sworn he wouldn't go anymore.

You wanted an excuse to see him.

No.

Danny would've gotten you out. He probably had some contact close by.

I'm not risking him unless I have to.

But you'll risk the man you love.

Simon wanted to rip something or someone apart.

Edgar knelt beside him and arranged his supplies on the coffee table. "This is going to hurt. Your shirt's embedded in the wound. If I could take you to my office…"

Simon shook his head. "Just do it."

He closed his eyes. He'd bear it somehow, but he wasn't going to watch. He was tired of hurting. He'd had much worse wounds than this one—like the ones that had almost killed him that cool morning off the coast of Africa. He pushed at the memories that threatened to take him back there. He could hear the rain, see flames engulfing the ship, feel Edgar's hands gripping him. But that wasn't real. Edgar was though, and now he was going to save Simon again.

Pain threatened to crush Simon and it wasn't coming from his wound. He worried that feeling Edgar's hands on him again might break him rather than heal him. Why was he so fucked up? His eyes burned. Was he really going to dissolve into tears like a fucking baby?

You've burned yourself out, pushed yourself to the limit.

Simon nodded to the voice in his head. He was going to die if he didn't get out, but he had to finish this. No way in hell was he going to stop until he'd found all the fuckers responsible for the death of his crewmembers on the *Ridgeway*, Sport and Jackson's teammates, and so many others.

Edgar laid a hand on his shoulder. "Are you okay?"

"No." Simon didn't have the strength to pretend otherwise.

Edgar spread a towel on the couch. "Come on. Lie down. I don't need you passing out on me."

Simon had been able to ignore his wound during the drive from Suffolk to Richmond—God it had

20

seemed endless. But the pain exploded as Edgar helped him recline. Part of him welcomed it, though. Physical pain was so much easier to handle than the agony that threatened to tear him up from the inside out.

"There," Edgar said. "Don't move or you'll bleed all over my fucking couch. It's not even a month old."

Simon almost smiled. Edgar always got grouchy when he was worried. If he really cared about the couch, he wouldn't have settled Simon there. Even with a towel under him, he'd likely ruin the upholstery when Edgar pulled the bullet out. Just one more thing he'd owe Edgar.

Edgar laid a hand on Simon's forehead. "You've lost a lot of blood. You're dehydrated and likely running a fever. I really wish we could do this at my office."

"Just fucking take care of it. That is what I came here for." Nothing pissed Simon off more than realizing how vulnerable he was. Edgar was right. He was in bad shape. He wouldn't have made it much farther without passing out.

"It's nice to see you too, Si."

"Goddammit, Edgar. They had me locked up for days, and I…" Panic hovered, threatening to overtake him. With the last of his strength, he pushed it away and sank deeper into the couch cushions, utterly exhausted.

The silence got to him after a few seconds. He managed to lift his eyelids, but even that movement was a strain. Edgar was studying him, pain and confusion in his hazel eyes. Why did Simon keep hurting this man when all he wanted to do was love him?

Edgar pushed Simon's hair back from his face and gave him a soft smile. "I've got this. Just relax and let me take care of you."

Simon nodded. If only it were that simple.

He sucked in his breath as Edgar began pulling his T-shirt away from his wound. He wanted to yell but instead bit his lip, holding it in. Edgar didn't need to deal with a baby.

"You okay?"

"Yes." He forced the word out through gritted teeth.

Edgar rolled his eyes. "No, you're not."

"Please."

"Simon, you've been shot. It's okay to admit it hurts."

Simon shook his head vigorously. And Edgar arched a brow.

Great. He'd gone from baby to petulant three-year-old. "It fucking hurts. Is that what you want to hear? Just get it done."

"Thank you, Edgar. I appreciate you letting me in even though I swore this wouldn't happen again, Edgar. You're so very helpful, Edgar."

"Fuck off."

Edgar pulled his shirt the rest of the way off his wound.

Simon gasped for breath.

"Go ahead. Curse me some more. I've got to tweeze the fabric out, extract the bullet, disinfect the wound, and sew it up."

"Fucking cocksucking son of a bitch! Don't you have any local anesthetic? What kind of doctor are you?"

"The kind who doesn't bring his office home."

Simon fought for breath as pain radiated across his torso. "Seriously? You've got nothing?"

"I'm not a field medic anymore," Edgar said, but he lifted a syringe and began filling it.

"Then what is that?" Simon asked.

"Shut up." A smile played at the corner of Edgar's mouth.

Simon didn't know whether to be outraged or happy as fuck that Edgar could still tease him. "You were messing with me."

"Yes I'm going to fucking numb it. I don't keep as much shit at home as I used to, but I'm still equipped for one of your visits."

Simon glared at him in mock anger. "That was cruel."

"No, actually not using the anesthetic would be cruel."

"You wouldn—" Simon bit down on the word as Edgar stabbed him with the needle and the cold burn shot through his veins. "Fuck! I forgot how much I hate that stuff."

"I didn't and don't tell me you haven't needed any recently."

"I'm charmed, remember? I can usually dodge bullets."

"Not this time, apparently."

No, this time he'd been too desperate to get away and he'd fucked up. "Don't worry. I'm still invincible."

Edgar shook his head. "I remember you dying."

"I remember you bringing me back."

Edgar gave him a sad smile as he picked up the tweezers.

***

Edgar pulled a glass from the cabinet and poured an extra-large dose of Bushmills for himself. He had no doubt Simon would be happier drunk off his ass, but he needed to rehydrate. Edgar poured him a glass of water, wishing he had some Gatorade to offer instead. By the time Edgar had finished stitching him up, Simon was disturbingly pale and out of it. Edgar had seen him in far worse shape physically, but he'd never seen Simon look as hopeless or as scared. What the hell had he gotten into this time?

Edgar glanced across the half wall that separated his kitchen and living room. Simon had his eyes closed, but he wasn't asleep. Edgar knew better. He was hiding. It might not happen tonight, but he damn well would get some answers out of Simon one way or another. Edgar was involved in Simon's mission-gone-wrong now whether he liked it or not.

He wished he had something stronger than ibuprofen to give Si. The local would wear off soon. Simon could take the pain, Edgar had no doubt about that, but he hated watching him suffer. Though the stubborn bastard would likely refuse drugs even if Edgar had them, saying he couldn't let himself be compromised. He wouldn't refuse a drink, though.

What Simon really needed was antibiotics. Edgar could easily get some from his office, but he didn't want to leave Si alone. He might be more deadly while wounded than most men in perfect health, but right now, he looked half dead.

Was Simon really that bad off or was it part of

his act? Edgar hated that he had to ask himself that. But Si had gotten so used to showing people what they needed or wanted to see. Edgar wasn't sure he could turn that off anymore. Either way, he wasn't leaving Simon alone, which meant he had to find someone to bring supplies to them.

He wasn't close to the other doctors in his practice. They were older and friendly enough, but he wouldn't trust them with a secret like Simon. Laura. Was she his best option? Laura's psychiatric practice shared a building with Edgar's internist group, so she had keys to the building and access to what Edgar needed. He could trust her. He was sure of that even though he'd only known her a few months. They'd become friends after a failed attempt at dating. She'd lost her husband a few months before moving to Richmond. Edgar hadn't exactly lost Simon, but he'd lost the will to fight for him. They'd spent a lot of time commiserating, though Edgar hadn't shared the details of his failed nonrelationship. Maybe he was a fool to bring her in on whatever Simon had gotten into, but he couldn't live like Simon and Danny, always expecting someone he met to stab him in the back.

Once he got Simon to sleep, he'd call Laura. No way would Simon agree to involve anyone else if he were awake. Edgar didn't want to put Laura in danger but she was a damn fine shot—they spent some enjoyable afternoons at the gun range—and she knew a little of Edgar's past so she wouldn't be overly shocked. She was also the only choice he had.

He poured a second glass of whiskey for Simon to drink after the water, balanced the three glasses in his hands, and walked back into the living room. He sat the glasses on the coffee table, knelt by the couch, and laid a hand on Simon's chest. "I know you aren't asleep. I've got water and whiskey. You'll get the latter after the former."

Simon opened his eyes and glared at Edgar. "Seriously? You're withholding alcohol when I've been shot."

"You're dehydrated. Water first."

Simon eyed the glasses of amber liquid. "Is that the good stuff?"

Edgar smiled. "Bushmills 21 Year-Old Single Malt."

"Fuck me."

"Not in that condition."

Simon made a sad puppy face. "Then can I at least have a bendy straw for my water?"

"Fuck no."

Simon sighed as if he were extremely put-upon. "What kind of doctor are you?"

Edgar ignored him. "Do you need me to help you sit up?"

Simon glared at him, but when he raised up to his elbows, he gasped. "Uh…"

Edgar shook his head. "Goddammit, Si. It won't kill you to have help." Edgar slipped a few pillows behind Simon's back. "I'd forgotten how awful you are when you're hurting."

"Fuck you. I'm not—"

Edgar glared at him. "Oh right, I'm sorry. You're not awful. You're *fucking* awful." Edgar chose that moment to lift Simon to a sitting position, knowing it would hurt like hell.

"Son of cockmonkey's donkey ass bitch!"

Edgar had to take a sip of his own drink to keep from laughing. Or worse, kissing Si. Why the hell Si's creative cursing turned him on, he had no idea.

How much longer are you going to keep him in the dark about how you feel?

For-fucking-ever.

Idiot.

He's my best friend. I can't screw that up.

Your dick sure as hell thinks he's more than a friend.

My dick can fuck off.

Not much of that lately. But wanting him isn't the problem, anyway. It's loving him that has you freaked.

Edgar took another sip of whiskey and sat the glass down. He couldn't deny it, at least not to himself. He was in love with Simon and had been for a long time. But Simon was sunny and charming, at least when he wasn't deep in a mission. And Edgar... Well, he knew his shit and he stitched people up so they could get their jobs done, but he wasn't going to win any personality contests.

He realized Simon was grinning at him.

"What?" Did he know? Edgar often worried he did and that he used it against Edgar. Fuck, maybe he actually wasn't any better at trusting people than Si.

Simon drank the last of his water and handed Edgar his glass. Edgar took it and gave him the whiskey. Simon took a sip and frowned. "I wish I could really enjoy this."

"I wish I had something cheaper to give you so it wasn't wasted."

"Only the finer things now that you're a fancy city doctor, huh?"

Edgar flipped him off.

Simon laid a hand on his arm. "You deserve it."

Edgar felt like he'd missed something. "What?"

"You deserve to have whatever you want."

"And you don't?"

Simon shook his head. "You're a good man."

"Si—" Edgar fucking hated when Si put himself down.

Simon held up a hand and downed the rest of his drink, making Edgar cringe at the thought of all that aged flavor doing nothing but burning Si's throat and sending him to sleep. Simon wasn't going to continue the conversation. This wasn't the first time they'd had it. Could Simon really believe he wasn't a good man, one of the best, after all he'd sacrificed for others?

Edgar took the glass from Si and covered him with the blanket he'd used earlier. "Get some sleep."

"I'll try. But…"

Edgar laid a hand on Si's shoulder. "But what?"

"Never mind."

Edgar wanted to know what he'd been about to say, but it was Si. If he didn't want to tell, he wouldn't, not even under torture.

CHAPTER THREE

Laura answered on the second ring. "Edgar? What's up?"

"I need to ask you a favor." *A really fucking big favor.*

"At six AM on Saturday?"

She was lucky he hadn't called earlier. "I needed to catch you before my office opens for the weekend clinic."

"O-kaaaay." She sounded even more skeptical than he'd anticipated. He wished he knew a good lead-in to his request.

"I need you to bring me a few things from the office and not mention it to anyone."

"What kind of things? Edgar, what's going on? Are you in some kind of trouble?"

"No. Um… a friend sort of is." *Oh my fuck that sounds pathetic.* "I need some antibiotics and pain meds."

Silence. He was fucking things up. He'd never been a smooth talker, not like Si and Danny. "I wish I could tell you more, but for now you're just going to have to trust me that there's nothing illegal, nothing you would object to going on."

"Just me stealing prescription drugs from the office?"

"Well, yeah, except that."

She exhaled loudly. "Edgar, you're going to have to do better than that."

"I'm treating someone. A friend from my days in the military. He was on an undercover op and things went sideways. I can't bring him into the office and risk him being seen. I don't want to leave him alone either. He's not in a position to defend himself." Simon would argue that point, but Edgar didn't care. He wasn't in any shape to be on his own.

"There's more to your Navy career than you've told me, isn't there?"

Edgar sighed. "I was the medic for a SEAL team, and then the Navy sent me to medical school. I served on a ship under the friend I'm helping now. After I got out, I did… some other things." After the sinking of the *Ridgeway*, the CIA had declared Simon dead, given him a new identity, and sent him on black ops missions. He put his own team together and Edgar had spent a few years working with him. He'd fucking hated it. "I can't explain more than that. I've said too much already."

"Your *friend* is hurt?"

She sounded like she wasn't sure there really was a friend.

"This isn't about me. You can meet him if you bring me what I need." Fuck, Simon was going to kill him.

"How much trouble am I walking into?"

Edgar ran a hand over his hair. He had to be honest, and that made him realize that this was crazy. He'd just have to leave Si and get the medicine himself. "I don't know. My friend doesn't think anyone tailed him here. Look, I'm asking too much.

Just—"

"No. It's okay. I'll do it."

"I can protect you while you're here, but—"

"I'm taking a risk, I get it. How badly is he hurt?"

She sounded far more confident now. Edgar should still tell her to forget it, but he didn't. "He's been shot in the side. Nothing vital was hit, but the bullet was in him for over a day so I'm worried about infection."

"Shit, that does sound bad."

"Yeah." All Edgar could do was agree.

"He should be in a hospital."

"That's not an option, but he's tough. He's been through worse."

Edgar could practically feel her shuddering through the phone. "Tell me what you need and give me about… forty-five minutes."

"Thank you." He ran through the list of supplies he needed to treat Simon and hung up. *Please, God, don't let me be putting Laura in danger.*

***

"Simon. Siiii-mon!"

Edgar's apartment. That's where he was. For a second he'd thought he was still… No. Not there. No chains. Fuck! It was a good thing Edgar knew not to touch him when he was sleeping.

"You awake now?"

His mouth was dry so he just grunted to let Edgar know he was more or less conscious.

"We're about to have a visitor. I want you awake."

Simon reached under his pillow, reflexively

searching for a weapon, but there wasn't one there.

This time Edgar did touch him, laying a hand on his arm. "A *friendly* visitor."

Simon flopped back against the pillow and groaned as the movement pulled at his side. "Fuck. I… I thought they'd found me."

"What are the chances of that? I don't want my friend walking into something that could turn ugly."

Simon hated that there was any chance at all. *Please don't let them find me.* It was bad enough he'd gone back on his word to Edgar. He didn't need to put him in danger too. "I took out a lot of them and they have other things to concentrate on, but they also really hate me."

Edgar rolled his eyes. "Yeah, I can imagine."

"I think we're safe, but I guess I better hide." He gasped as he levered himself up to a sitting position. "Fuck, I'm sore."

"No shit. You do actually have a gunshot wound. And no hiding. Laura's bringing antibiotics and Percocet for you."

Laura? Who the hell is this Laura? "I can't believe you told someone I was here."

"I didn't reveal your darkest secrets or anything, but I had to tell her something. You need antibiotics and I'm not leaving you."

"Fine. But no pain pills. As soon as I have antibiotics, I'm out of here." No way was he going to endanger Edgar longer than he had to.

"The fuck you are. This isn't a drive-through medical facility." Edgar looked as angry as Si had ever seen him. What the fuck was that about? Edgar hadn't wanted him there in the first place.

"I know that, bu—"

"Do you? Really? Because I don't think you do."

Now Simon was pissed. Earlier he'd thought Edgar had forgiven him, that maybe… God, he'd wanted his friend back and now Edgar was being a fucking bastard. "I'm so sorry I can't stick around and enjoy your hospitality, but I happen to be in the middle of a mission."

"Aren't you always?"

"What the fuck does that mean?"

Someone knocked on the door, interrupting Edgar before he could respond, not that he'd likely intended to explain himself. "Edgar, it's me. Laura," the person at the door called.

"Try not to act like an ass to her no matter how pissed you are at me." Edgar spat the words at him and Simon was seriously tempted to punch him in his fucking steely-jawed craggy face. The son of a bitch.

Fortunately for both of them, Edgar turned away before Simon's urge overtook him.

**

Edgar grabbed his gun on the way to the door just in case someone had been lying in wait and they were holding Laura at gunpoint, forcing her to knock and announce herself. Fucking hell, a few hours with Si and he was already acting like an operative who constantly had to look over his shoulder.

He couldn't see anyone besides Laura, but he still kept his gun in his hand as he opened the door. He ushered a wide-eyed Laura in, glanced down the hall both ways, then tucked the gun into the back of his waistband.

"You get everything?" he asked as he shut the

door.

Laura stared at him for a few seconds. "That was… unexpected. I'm not used to you playing commando."

"Trust me. He's not playing. He may not look like it, but I promise you he's quite the badass when he wants to be." Simon had raised himself to a seated position without making a sound. That had to have hurt like hell.

"And what about you, are you equally dangerous?" Laura asked.

"Oh, I'm much worse," Simon said, giving his sunniest smile. He looked like a blond god, like the sort of man women would walk into hell for. Edgar expected Laura to fall under his spell immediately, but his charms didn't seem to work on her.

"Laura, this is Simon. Simon, this is Dr. Laura Hazelwood." Simon nodded to show he'd heard, but he glared at Edgar, probably pissed as hell that Edgar had used his real name. Not that the name would show on any ID he'd carried in the last five years. Simon McLeod was dead.

"Just how much trouble have you brought down on Edgar?" Laura asked.

She sounded pissed. Almost as pissed as Edgar ought to be, but of course, Simon's charms worked wonders on Edgar. He was thoroughly under Simon's spell. Even months apart hadn't changed that.

Simon gave her a once-over, then nodded approvingly. "I see why Edgar counts you as a friend."

"Maybe it's because I don't put his life in danger."

"He doesn't expect any better from me. Right, dear?" Simon looked at Edgar with a saccharine smile, but Edgar saw the hurt in his eyes.

"I…"

Laura saved him from answering by pulling a bag from her massive purse. Was she also hiding an assault rifle in there? "Here are the meds you need." She set them down on the coffee table, then turned to look at Edgar. "It seems like you're rather close to the patient. Do you want a second opinion on how bad off he is?"

***

"No," Simon said, just as Edgar said, "Yes."

Laura glanced between the two of them. Simon didn't want to be examined. He just wanted her to leave. "Edgar's patched me up countless times. In fact, I died and he brought me back to life. Three times. I trust him."

Edgar scowled at Si, obviously confused by why he was being so snippy. Simon didn't really get it himself except that Laura was beautiful and successful and not an operative, not someone who would expect Edgar to patch him up at three AM before disappearing again. Laura was what he needed. And Simon hated it. Were the two of them dating? Would Edgar have told him?

"Goddammit, Simon, I was half asleep when you showed up and… Just let her check you out."

"I don't want to. You know what you're doing." He sounded three years old. Again. Why the fuck did Edgar bring out his most petty self?

Laura sat on the couch next to Simon. "You're right. Edgar's an excellent doctor, but our skills are compromised when we work on patients we care about."

"Not true for a field medic."

"He's not a field medic anymore."

No, he was in Laura's world now. "So you work together?" Simon asked, wanting to stall some more.

"Kind of," Laura said.

Simon looked at Edgar, wanting more of an explanation.

"She works in the office next to mine. She's a psychiatrist."

A fucking shrink? "What the hell is she doing examining me, then?"

Laura raised her brows. "Psychiatrists do go to medical school. I did a residency and everything before going on to my specialty."

"She also volunteers at a free clinic, so she has more recent general medical experience."

Of course she does.

Laura knelt by the couch and Simon pulled back the blanket he'd covered himself with. He was still wearing his blood-stained cargo pants, but he hadn't bothered trying to put on a shirt after Edgar had cut his off. That would have been unnecessarily painful. Laura's eyes widened as she looked at his torso. Simon assumed her expression was a mix of appreciation for the muscles he'd worked damn hard for and horror at the number of scars he carried.

"My job's a rough one, Dr. Hazelwood."

She met his gaze briefly. "I see that."

"Si, just let her do her job," Edgar begged.

"And what is her job? To screw with my head?" What the fuck was wrong with him? Laura had taken a risk to bring him medicine. Could he blame it on the fever? His side sure as hell felt like it was on fire. He shook his head in answer to his own question. He was lucid enough not to be an ass. "I'm sorry."

Edgar whistled. "Laura, you should feel honored. I'm not sure I've ever heard Simon apologize."

Simon barely stopped himself from sticking his tongue out at Edgar.

Laura's hands were cool and gentle as she checked his wound, but they didn't give him the sense of comfort that Edgar's did. He doubted anyone else could make him feel that safe.

Laura leaned back and looked at Edgar. "Looks good, but I'm glad I brought the antibiotics." She shifted her gaze to Si. "What have you taken for pain?"

Simon shook his head. "Nothing."

Laura studied him. "I'm impressed if that's what you're going for."

"It hurts like fuck, okay? But I need to be fully present."

"You aren't fully present if you're in pain."

"I can do anything I have to as long as my head is clear." *Except tell Edgar how I feel.*

"I've seen him beat three-on-one odds more injured than this," Edgar said. Heat rose in Simon's cheeks. Edgar defending him made him fucking giddy.

Laura nodded. "Okay, then."

"Thank you, Laura," Edgar said. Was he ready for her to go? Simon shouldn't be so pleased with that. Of course he was probably just trying to keep her safe.

"Yeah, thanks," Simon added.

She looked at him with an expression that said she saw more of him than he wanted her to. "You're welcome." She stood and picked up her purse. "Walk me out?" she asked Edgar.

"Sure." Edgar smiled and took her arm. *The bastard.* What really made Simon want to yell or smash something—or maybe beat the shit out of Edgar—was that there was no reason for him to dislike Laura other than insane jealousy. How could he resent their relationship when he didn't have the nerve to tell Edgar how he felt, especially when he had no hope that Edgar, his straight friend, felt the same way?

He closed his eyes and thought about an escape plan.

CHAPTER FOUR

Edgar opened the door and Laura stepped into the hallway. "Is he the one?" she asked, keeping her voice to a whisper.

He frowned. "The one what?"

"The person who broke your heart. You never did actually say it was a woman, you know."

Edgar made a strangled noise and turned it into a cough. Of course she'd picked up on that.

Laura grinned. "I thought so."

"No." Edgar tried to look angry rather than frightened. "What the hell? I don't…"

She raised her brows. "Please. Do you think I'm blind? The way he reacted, defending you and then getting all territorial."

Edgar groaned. No, she damn well wasn't blind. She saw dynamics most people never noticed. "He's always like that."

"Uh-huh." Laura laughed. "I wish you luck."

"Laura, this isn't—"

"It *isn't* a lot of things, but you need to get back in there and figure out what it *is*."

What the fuck had he been thinking inviting a psychiatrist over? He should have gotten the damn drugs himself. "Laura, I don't want to argue about this."

She glared at him in what he hoped was mock

anger. "I just broke into your office and stole meds for you. The least you can do is not insult my intelligence."

Edgar sighed. No way in hell was he going to convince her he didn't have feelings for Si that went beyond friendship. "Simon has no idea how I feel."

Laura grinned. "I wouldn't be so sure."

"He thinks I'm straight."

Laura studied him as if waiting for more information.

"I was until Simon, until our friendship shifted somehow. I don't fucking know how it happened, but I swear he has no idea."

"Maybe not, but he certainly knows how he feels about you."

"Whatever he feels isn't strong enough to keep him here."

Laura studied Edgar so carefully he wondered if she was reading his thoughts. He hoped to hell not. "You mean his feelings aren't strong enough to make him change for you?"

Edgar scowled, hating that she was right. But no matter how much she thought she knew, he could never explain the history between him and Si. "You don't get it. There's so much between us that I can't talk about."

Laura had the decency to look contrite. "I probably shouldn't have said that, or any of this."

"Damn right."

"However, it's said and there's no going back. You asked me for a favor and I'm asking you for one in return. Tell him how you feel before he leaves."

"What?" Edgar's chest tightened until it was hard

to draw in air. "I…" He couldn't, could he?

And yet, how can you not? How can you let him walk away again?

"At least think about it."

He nodded, mouthed a thank-you, and shut the door. He laid his head against the solid wood, trying to get his equilibrium back.

"What the fuck was that about?" Simon asked, an angry edge to his voice.

"Just… um… some work shit."

Simon's expression said he didn't believe Edgar for a second, but he didn't ask any more questions.

Was Simon jealous like Laura thought? Should Edgar reassure him if he was? He watched Simon as he sat on Edgar's now blood-stained couch. His gaze drifted to the bandage Laura had placed back over the stitches. How many more times would Edgar sew Simon up after he put his life on the line because some idiot at the CIA had taken advantage of Simon's belief that he was invincible? They were never going to stop asking Simon to do things no one else would agree to if he never learned to say no.

Edgar hated how his heart hammered from nothing more complicated than looking at Simon. The little bastard managed to make Edgar both angry and afraid without doing a fucking thing.

"You didn't really mean that earlier, did you?" Simon asked, his voice soft and… sad? While there'd been glimpses of his usual sass, Simon wasn't himself, and Edgar knew him well enough to know that wasn't just because he'd been shot. What the hell had happened to him to throw him off his game?

"Mean what?"

"About me staying. I can go now. I'll take the meds."

Edgar shook his head. Simon wouldn't remember. He sucked at taking care of himself. "No, you won't."

"I'll try." He grinned, looking more like himself, like the seductive little shit confident of getting everyone to do his bidding.

No, Edgar was not going to reassure him. He didn't give a fuck if Simon was jealous or not. In fact, maybe he'd make damn sure Si had something to be jealous about so Edgar could watch him squirm. Si wasn't leaving until he was healed. After that… Did he dare take Laura's advice? She was good at her job, ridiculously good, but… Hell, if he were honest, he'd been thinking about telling Simon anyway or just shoving him up against a wall and kissing him until Si had no more doubts where the two of them stood. He'd get a hell of a lot of satisfaction from how that would shock Si.

Was there any point in hiding how he felt anymore? If Simon opened his damn eyes and really looked at him, he'd see Edgar's feelings as clearly as Laura did. Usually Simon could read people almost as well as she could, but he'd had always been shit at reading Edgar. Maybe Edgar could keep hiding what he wanted, but he was tired of it. He'd hoped that telling Si to fuck off would help, that if they weren't talking all the time, if Simon didn't show up unexpectedly, wounded, drunk, wanting something, then Edgar would forget about wanting to kiss his full, pouty lips or to stroke that… Fuck, why the hell did he have to realize he craved Si more than he'd ever craved anything before?

Without speaking to Simon, Edgar opened the bag Laura had placed on the table and extracted a bottle of intravenous antibiotics and a syringe.

Simon scowled at him. "I want pills."

"You're getting this. It'll work much faster."

"Fuck no, those shots hurt worse than a bullet."

Edgar arched a brow. "Shift over onto your side."

Simon's eyes narrowed, and he pursed his lips. "Do you really hate me this much?"

Edgar shrugged. "Some days."

Simon huffed, but he rolled over so Edgar could inject the medicine into the top of his ass. He spewed a litany of curse words but otherwise cooperated.

"There, all done. Now you're going to take your nice pain pills and I'll take you to bed."

Simon huffed. "You've stabbed me and now you're going to knock me out and take advantage of me."

Edgar used a more serious tone. "Si. You're staying and you should sleep somewhere nicer than the couch."

Simon looked up at him. No matter how much time Edgar spent around Simon, he never stopped marveling at the intense blue of Simon's eyes. He could look into them for hours.

Ugh. What a sickeningly romantic thought.

It's true, though.

Fuck off.

Simon shook his head. "I should go. I swore I wouldn't put you in danger again." His beautiful eyes shimmered. Was he about to fucking cry? Edgar put a hand to Simon's forehead. He didn't feel any hotter than he had before. Edgar laid two fingers against Simon's wrist and checked his pulse. Rapid but not alarmingly so. "Are you okay?"

Simon held Edgar's gaze for a few seconds. Then he looked away and shook his head.

"Talk to me."

"I can't."

Edgar wanted to push. He would get the story out of Simon whether it was fucking classified or not. But Simon should sleep first, give the meds time to start working.

Edgar pulled out the bottle of painkiller.

"No," Simon insisted. "Just give me another drink."

"Si, you need something stronger."

"No," he shouted, immediately looking embarrassed by his vehemence. "Alcohol won't fuck with me like that shit."

Edgar sighed, allowing himself to look defeated by Si's argument, but he had a plan. Si was too fucking stubborn and he'd had enough. Si had shown up wanting help, he was going to fucking get it.

Simon swung his legs off the couch and tried to stand. "Fuck, that hurts. I walked ten miles and drove for over an hour and it didn't hurt this bad."

"Adrenaline kept you going, Si. It's out of your system now."

Simon scowled. "Fucking right it is. Are you gonna help me up or what?"

"Oh, does the captain require assistance?" Edgar went so far as to flutter his lashes for effect.

"Does the doctor want me to tear my stitches open?" Simon's words were tight, his face pale. He really was in pain, but Edgar was still pissed and he *had* offered the bastard pain meds.

"I hardly think walking will—"

"Not walking. I'm going to rip them out punching the good doctor in the fucking face."

Edgar laughed. "Quit being a baby." He slid his arm under Si's and helped him up.

Simon pushed him away once he was on his feet. "I'm good."

One step and he had to steady himself on a chair.

"Just let me help. I know you could walk if you had to, okay? If someone broke in here right now, you'd take them out like you didn't feel a fucking thing. I've seen you do it. But right now, I can help you walk with less pain. Let me."

Simon gave a curt nod, and Edgar put an arm around him. He leaned on Edgar more heavily than Edgar would have expected. Edgar did not like how warm and dry his skin felt. He prayed the antibiotic Laura grabbed at the office would be strong enough to beat the infection, but he worried it wouldn't. And he was just as concerned about Si's mental state.

"Si, this is bad, isn't it?" he asked, hoping to distract Simon from the pull on his side that came with every step.

"I've had worse." Edgar could hear the pain in his voice, though, physical and emotional.

"You're right about the bullet wound, but that's not the only thing hurting you. Something about this mission has fucked you up."

Simon stiffened. "I'm fine."

"Right. Of course you are."

Simon blew out a harsh breath. "I will be when

this is over."

When would it ever be over? When Si was dead?

Simon sat on the edge of the bed, leaning toward his good side, supporting himself on his arm. He looked like he might collapse any second. "You're giving me your bed?"

"I'll be fine on the couch." Edgar had rented a one-bedroom apartment when he'd moved to Richmond since he intended to look for a house, but he'd never actually gotten motivated to move. He reached behind himself and eased a syringe filled with a sedative from his pocket while Simon caught his breath. If Simon were at full strength, he'd never get away with what he'd planned, but Si needed sleep and Edgar was going to see that he got it.

Lightning fast, he put Si in a chokehold and jabbed the syringe into his arm. Simon tried to claw his way free, but Edgar held on and depressed the plunger. Si freed himself as the last of the drug went into his body. Edgar stumbled back, and Si jerked the syringe from his arm and threw it across the room.

"Son of a fucking bitch, what did you do?"

Edgar smiled, proud of himself for getting the upper hand for once. "Guaranteed that you'd get some sleep."

Simon took a step toward him and faltered. He scrubbed his hands over his face. "Fuck, how strong was it?"

"Strong enough to put you down."

"Why?" Si looked scared, and Edgar felt a touch of remorse. Si really did hate being out of control.

"Because someone has to take care of you."

Anger flashed in Simon's eyes. He took a few

more steps before his legs started to buckle. Edgar grabbed him before he hit the floor.

"I want to hate you," Si said, his words slurred.

Edgar helped Si back to bed. "Then hate me, but I'm not going to let you kill yourself, at least not tonight."

"Can't—"

"You can die, Si. I watched you do it, and I can't always be there to bring you back."

"No, can't hate you, 'cause I love you."

Edgar sucked in his breath. Had he heard Si right?

He's high on that shit you pumped into him. He'd say anything.

Yeah, like the truth.

No. That couldn't be the truth. Well, it could, but Simon loves you as a friend, nothing more.

Keep fooling yourself. And you'll tear both of you apart.

He tucked Simon in and sat on the edge of the bed watching him, the rise and fall of his chest, his beautiful full lips, his golden hair that didn't look out of place despite all he'd been through. Edgar's chest ached. He wanted Simon in a way he'd never wanted anyone else. He wished to God he didn't, and not because Simon was a man. He'd be damned if he'd listened to any prejudiced bullshit about who he loved. But he doubted Simon was capable of loving one man, and he sure as hell wasn't capable of settling down. Edgar wanted the dream—a house with a picket fence, a dog or two, and someone to share it with. Simon would laugh at him for even thinking about such a life. He'd swear Edgar would be bored in no time.

You're already bored.
I'm lonely, that's not the same.
You miss the team.
But not the danger.
Maybe there's a compromise.
Simon McLeod doesn't compromise.

CHAPTER FIVE

Si lay perfectly still as he tried to remember where he was. His side ached, but he was on a soft mattress. His head felt… full of cotton. Concussion? No. At least he didn't think so. The room smelled like… Edgar.

That brought the memories back. He'd been shot. He'd come to Edgar who had patched him up and then… drugged him. Edgar had fucking drugged him.

He pushed up onto his elbows and cursed as the movement pulled at his side.

That's what you get for waiting so long to get help.

Like I had a choice.

There's always a choice.

Not if you want to protect other people.

Sometimes, maybe, you could protect yourself.

I did. I came to the one person I could trust and he screwed me over.

"Edgar?" No response. "Edgar!" He forced himself up as he scanned the room for a weapon. Then he heard footsteps.

"Si, I'm here. It's okay." Edgar appeared in the doorway drenched in sweat, wearing only a pair of gym shorts. "I was working out. I didn't hear you at first."

Si couldn't decide what he wanted to do more:

tell Edgar off for what he'd done or relieve him of his minimal clothing and taste the thick cock he could see outlined through them. Damn, Edgar was hot like that—sweaty, worn out, hazel eyes sparkling. Edgar might have given up fieldwork, but he hadn't gone soft, that was for damn sure. Simon wanted to run his hands over Edgar's firm pecs and feel the rasp of hair on his fingers. He wanted to hold onto Edgar's shoulders while Edgar claimed him, owned him. Wait... where the hell had that come from? Simon shook his head. The drugs must still be fucking with him.

He remembered waking or half waking a few times. Edgar had been there. He'd forced Simon to drink more water. Had he made him eat too? Simon wasn't sure what he'd dreamed and what was reality. He hoped to God he hadn't said anything to Edgar about wanting him. He'd sure had some powerful dreams about Edgar—naked, in bed, giving Si what he craved.

"Are you okay?" Edgar asked.

Simon scowled at him. "No. You fucking drugged me. How long did I sleep?"

"Since I last woke you to keep you hydrated or since I sedated you for medical reasons?"

Simon flipped him off. "Fucker. You know I mean the whole damn time. How long have I been out of it?"

Edgar tilted his head and studied Simon for a moment. "A while."

"Edgar, don't fucking mess with me."

"Thirteen hours, give or take."

Fucking fuck. "Are you going to attack me again

if I try to leave now?"

"I doubt I'll get the jump on you a second time, but I'll try. I could always just shoot you."

"You wouldn't." He wouldn't, would he?

"If I were going to, I'd have done it before now. Like you said, you give people a lot of reasons."

Every minute Simon stayed with Edgar gave the men he'd eluded more time to track him and that put Edgar in danger. But Edgar was right—the fucker—Simon didn't have the strength to make it far, certainly not to DC, which was where he needed to go. He and Danny had to make a plan. He'd told Danny only the barest of essentials. He'd been unsure how secure their communications were. Of course if… No, Edgar wasn't going to help him. Or maybe… "I need some things if I'm going to stay here."

"You sure as fuck do. Rest. Water. Food."

"I'm with you on the food. I'm fucking starving."

"That's a good sign." Edgar sat on the side of the bed, and Simon's cock responded to his scent: sweaty, musky, coffee-flavored fuckability. Edgar laid a hand on Simon's forehead. "Cooler. I think the antibiotic is working. How do you feel?"

Like fucking you. He could grab Edgar, flip him over, pin him, and then… Okay, maybe he was still feverish if he was thinking this way. The last time he'd been around Edgar, he hadn't been this fucking horny, had he? Was that why he'd run? No, he'd run because Edgar had sent him away. And rightly so. Simon had acted like a self-important asshole who couldn't be bothered to think about anyone else.

"Fine. I feel fucking fine. I need a phone, a secure laptop or one I can make secure, a bacon cheeseburger, sweet potato fries, and doughnuts, lots of doughnuts." Edgar expected him to be an ass so that's what he'd be.

Edgar stared at him with a look of disbelief. "You're serious?"

"About the phone and shit? Yeah."

"About the food?"

"Well, it's a start."

"Si—"

"Look, I haven't really eaten in… a long fucking time."

Edgar huffed, but Si thought he was actually pleased Simon was feeling like his imperious self. "I'm not driving all over town to satisfy your whims," Edgar protested.

Simon pouted, knowing how it would get to Edgar.

Edgar scowled. "Don't even try that pitiful lost puppy routine on me. That won't help you get your way, Si."

Simon knew better. Edgar had never been able to resist his act, especially if he added bribery to the mix. "I was captured and shot and then drugged by my best friend. I deserve a burger and doughnuts. If you get what I need, I might even give you a straight answer to a few of your questions."

"Oh my fucking God, Si. You will tell me what you've been up to, what you learned, what has you spooked. All of it."

Simon nodded. "Okay."

"Seriously? You're not going to argue."

He shouldn't tell him a fucking thing, but just like Simon knew Edgar well enough to predict that he'd get Simon whatever he wanted no matter how much driving it involved, Edgar knew Simon would eventually make a full confession. "Bring me what I want and I'll tell you most of it."

Edgar fisted his hands. Simon wondered if he'd gone too far. Edgar looked like he was contemplating wrapping his hands around Simon's neck. "I really ought to fucking shoot you."

"Oh, and get some coffee. I really need some coffee." Maybe Edgar was right and Simon did have a death wish.

"I have plenty of coffee. You can make it yourself while I'm gone. And when I'm back, you'll tell me everything. Every fucking thing."

Simon would. "We'll see."

Edgar ignored that. "You can use my laptop, my personal one. But considering your track record with tech, you'll fuck it up. Does this mission have a budget?"

"What do you care? Aren't you a rich doctor?"

"Most family practice doctors aren't exactly rich. I can pay my bills, but I'm not supplying you with a steady stream of laptops to blow up."

"I'll see if I can get some government agency or another to pay you back for anything I destroy."

Edgar rolled his eyes. "Ha."

"Please." Simon gave the boyish smile that did most people in.

"I shouldn't leave you alone."

"I'm doing a lot better, honest. Just give me a gun. The bastards who captured me took my favorite Sig."

Edgar laid the back of his hand on his forehead

and pretended to swoon. "Oh no. What a tragedy."

"Don't mock me." This time the pouting was real. "You know how personal guns are."

"Too personal for you. That Sig was like your best friend."

Simon nodded. "Exactly."

Edgar shook his head. "There's a place down the street where I can fulfill your dinner order. I can get Krispy Kreme and the rest at a convenience store."

"Avoid the security cameras."

Edgar huffed. "You want me to take my gun along and shoot them out or what?"

Simon considered the suggestions. "Do you think you can get away with that?"

Edgar rolled his eyes. "I'll pay cash and be as invisible as possible. I know the drill."

"So you're in?" Simon asked. Maybe Edgar really would help him and Danny.

"No. I'm doing a favor for a friend because I'm a fucking sucker."

"You're amazing."

"Don't even try to flatter me." Edgar stomped from the room, but he returned a few seconds later with a gun—his backup Glock—for Simon as well as a throwing knife and a grenade.

Simon looked at his mini arsenal. "What the fuck? I thought you were a mild-mannered doctor now?"

Edgar shrugged. "It never hurts to be prepared."

"Yeah, you're a real Boy Scout," Simon said, fondling the knife. It was perfectly balanced.

"Compared to you, I sure as hell am."

"Go get my fucking doughnuts."

"Aye, aye, Captain." Edgar saluted him and turned to go.

***

Edgar's errands took longer than he would have liked. He couldn't bring himself to buy all the supplies Simon needed at one store because he'd been taught paranoia by the best. When he finally drove away from the pickup window at Buster's Burgers, Simon had been alone for two hours. Edgar drove quickly, but not recklessly. The last thing he needed was to get stopped by the police since he didn't exactly have the proper permits for some of the weapons he had with him. Being a former SEAL medic only got you so far.

At last he pulled into a parking place and raced up the stairs to his second-floor apartment. No sign of any trouble, and he could smell coffee. Simon had obviously made himself some. "Si?" he called once he got the door open.

"I'm in bed like a good little boy," Simon responded.

Edgar shook his head. When Simon started being a good little boy, he'd know the end of the world was nigh.

He set the food down and looked around for his laptop, figuring Simon could get started while he got plates out and served the food. It wasn't on the coffee table where he'd left it.

"I've already got the computer," Simon called.

Of course he did. He'd always made himself at home when he visited Edgar, not that Edgar wanted it any other way. They'd been as close as men could get without being lovers, surviving together, being prisoners together. He'd happily share anything with Simon, no matter what he'd told Simon when he sent him away months ago.

He wasn't prepared for the sight that assaulted him when he stepped into his bedroom. Simon was sitting up in his bed with a stack of pillows behind him, wearing an ancient cardigan of Edgar's over one of his T-shirts and a pair of reading glasses he must have found in the nightstand.

"What are you doing?" he asked Si.

"Working. What does it look like?"

"You're wearing my glasses. And my sweater."

"I was cold and it's not like I've got clothes of my own here."

"And the glasses?" Edgar asked.

Simon huffed. "So my eyes aren't perfect anymore. I get my job done."

Edgar pressed his lips together to keep from laughing. "I'm sure you do," he said when he could trust himself to keep a straight face.

"You're mocking me."

"No, not at all." But the laugh came through then. "You're the deadliest man I know, and here you are looking like a teenage dork in oversized clothes."

Simon shrugged. "I can't kill people all the time."

Edgar knew what a privilege it was to see this side of Simon since very few people ever did. The man in his bed was bookish, intelligent, unconcerned with what others thought of him. True he was a killer and the type of leader men would follow no matter how crazy the mission, but he had a nerdy side he rarely showed. And that made Edgar love him all the more.

Simon looked at him over the edge of his reading glasses. Edgar wanted to drop the bag of electronics, crawl into bed with him, and fuck his brains out.

Tell him how you feel. Laura's words echoed in Edgar's mind.

Not now. This isn't the right time.

"The glasses suit you, actually."

"They do?"

Edgar nodded, suddenly very uncomfortable. "Here's the stuff you asked for. I got a few things for you to wear since my clothes don't exactly fit." He dropped the bag on the bed. "Do what you need to with these, and I'll get out some plates."

Simon nodded, already focused on the laptop again.

"You want to eat in here or in the kitchen?"

"Oh, you got the burgers?"

Edgar shook his head. Had Si listened to anything he'd said? "Yes, with bacon, cheddar, and jalapeños just like you like them."

Simon groaned, the sound too sexual for Edgar's sanity. He backed away from the bed, hating how easily he reacted to Simon.

"And doughnuts?" Simon asked.

"Yes, glazed and cream-filled." Edgar realized that was a mistake. Watching Simon eat a cream-filled doughnut might just kill him.

"My savior." Simon laid a hand on his heart.

Edgar snorted.

"I need to make a call and then I'll come eat in the kitchen. I don't want to get crumbs in your bed."

"Fuck no. You better not." Edgar had plans for

that bed and he was growing more certain by the second that he was going to enact them all and to hell with the chances of ruining their friendship.

CHAPTER SIX

Simon pulled out the burner phone Edgar had brought him and called Danny. A very limited number of people could contact Danny on this particular line. Danny didn't answer, probably being cautious because he didn't recognize the number. Simon left a voicemail and tried not to worry.

The phone rang just as Simon was about to give up and go eat.

"What's up? Where are you?" Danny asked when he answered.

"You got my message?"

"Yes. What the fuck, Si? You leave me a message that you're on the run and then you drop off the face of the Earth. I've been trying to reach you for details, but—"

"I was shot. I'm safe now. Derrick sent me in and things went from too-good-to-be-true to goatfuck in under five seconds."

"Why the fuck didn't you bring me in?" Simon could hear the anger in Danny's voice.

"Too risky."

"Risk is my fucking life, Si."

"It was a one-man mission."

Danny huffed. "Apparently not. Where are you now?"

"The only place I could go." He was as sure as he

could be that the line was secure, but he still wouldn't say Edgar's name.

"We need to talk? How sure are you that he's our guy?"

"Really fucking sure." Simon had recognized Kingsford's voice. Kingsford, the fucking admiral who'd given him his command. "He's got an impressive number of troops where I was being held, and from what I heard, they aren't the only installation. The men are strong and well-trained."

"Fuck. So you think this really has been about a military coup all along?"

There was Irish in Danny's voice. That meant he was scared. Simon was too. "That's certainly fucking likely."

"You heading this way?" Danny asked.

"No. There's a lake house close to where I was held in Suffolk that they referred to as The Retreat. Kingsford owns it, though I doubt his name is on the deed. I heard talk of 'research' being done there. We need to check it out."

"Won't they have cleared out now that you know where it is?"

Simon paced the length of the room, wishing he had a solid plan. "Maybe, but I'm not sure they realized how much I put together. No matter what, we've got to try. And we'll need reinforcements."

"I'll manage as many of us as I can. Where do we meet?"

Would Edgar let them use his lake house? It was close to Kingsford's house. "Remember two years ago? Our headquarters?"

"That works. I'll send an ETA to this number."

Thank God Danny wasn't going to argue.

"I'll update if things change."

"Are things good there?" Danny's tone was uncharacteristically tentative.

"I think so."

"Is he joining us?"

Simon hated how scared he was that Edgar would stay behind. "I haven't sold that yet."

Danny snorted. "Good luck."

Simon ended the call. He was going to need it. He was certain Edgar would let them coordinate the mission at his lake house, especially once he knew what they were after. But when Simon told Edgar the classified intel from the mission, Edgar might be angry enough to join them. Edgar had sworn after they'd been taken prisoner in South America that he'd never go into the field again. But they needed him because he thought differently than the rest of the team. Jackson, Sport, and Danny were all as stubborn as Si. They all wanted to run things themselves. Could they be a team? Maybe, but they needed someone who wasn't determined to rush in, guns blazing, and blow everyone the fuck away if things went sideways. Jackson's boyfriend, Addy, would do that, but Edgar had the skills to defend himself and Addy didn't. Edgar could play in this world. He'd just burned out on it.

And so have you.

Not yet. Not until this is over.

But could Simon really walk away from this life? He'd never thought he would. After his ship had blown up and Edgar fought to keep him alive, he was certain he'd be in this until it truly killed him. But now… What was he thinking? He didn't deserve a quiet little life. Not after the things he'd done. How the hell could he fit into a community? And what would he do in the "real" world? Play housewife for Edgar? He shook his head, barely resisting the urge to throw his phone across the room.

He found Edgar in the kitchen. There were two plates at the table with huge burgers on them. The doughnuts were on the counter. Simon was a pain in the ass, but Edgar spoiled him anyway. He grabbed a doughnut and crammed half of it in his mouth.

"You'll ruin your dinner," Edgar scolded as he shut the fridge and carried the ketchup to the table.

Simon grabbed a second doughnut as he polished off the first. "No chance of that. I'm seriously starving."

"Fucking hell, when *was* the last time you ate?"

Simon shrugged.

"Why didn't you tell me you were hungry this morning?"

Simon poured himself a cup of coffee while he finished chewing. "I was busy not bleeding to death and you were busy fussing over me."

"I would have fed you."

"You drugged me before you had a chance."

Edgar glared at him.

"I didn't feel like eating then. I lifted a few energy bars while I was making my way here, so I wasn't dying or anything."

Edgar scowled at him. "Si—"

Simon held up his hand. "Don't. I need to talk to you."

"Yes, you do. What the fuck is going on?"

"It's classified." Simon couldn't resist snarking. It was his best defense when Edgar made him feel vulnerable.

Edgar slammed his hand down on the table. "Don't give me that crap. I know you've been running private jobs or doing crazy-ass shit on your own because nothing gives you a hard-on like doing the impossible."

"Well, not many things do." He looked pointedly at Edgar. "But this job was fully CIA-sanctioned, or at least that's what I was led to believe."

Edgar frowned. "You're working with Derrick again?"

Simon nodded. "I am, but he's been compromised."

Confusion showed on Edgar's face. "Then why…? What's going on?"

"You've missed a lot in the last few months." Butterflies dive-bombed each other in Simon's stomach. He couldn't do this without Edgar. This next mission would fucking end him if he didn't have support. Most people already thought he was crazy, and maybe he was, but he was afraid of how far he would go to make sure the men responsible for sinking the *Ridgeway* paid for what they'd done. But afterward… Simon was afraid he'd fall apart. He wasn't as tough as he pretended. Edgar knew that in a way no one else did. Simon needed Edgar to steady him.

"I've got a lead on the man who allowed the attack on the *Ridgeway*." The shock on Edgar's face was just what Simon expected.

"Are you fucking serious?"

"Yes. I'm guessing you know Rodriguez is dead."

Edgar nodded. "Yeah, I put that together when I heard what went down in North Carolina and saw Jackson's name."

Rodriguez had worked for a major Columbian drug cartel. He'd led an attack on a village and the SEAL team who was there to protect them from rebels. Jackson had been the team's leader, and the attack left him with a bum leg and one of his men dead. "Danny sent me to watch Addy while he kept tabs on Jackson's former teammate at the FBI."

"Cranford?"

Simon nodded. "He and Danny are lovers now."

Edgar choked on the bite of burger he'd just taken. After a long fit of coughing, he took a sip of his soda and cleared his throat. "What the fuck?"

Simon grinned. "They're perfect for each other."

"Danny? Danny has a… a boyfriend?"

"He does and it's serious."

Edgar's eyes widened as if he'd realized something. "That's why you didn't pull him in for whatever fiasco just earned you a bullet."

Simon nodded. "Right. And Jackson has a boyfriend too—Addy. He's not military or CIA, so he's a liability. At least Sport is as capable as Danny."

Edgar raised a brow. "Does Danny admit that?"

"More or less, and they have different skill sets." Danny would actually admit no such thing, and Sport would be pissed as hell to be told he was "as good as Danny." He'd say he was way fucking better.

"Okay, get to the point." Edgar never was one for patience.

"I helped Danny with a mission about six months ago. He needed a babysitter for Jackson's boyfriend."

Edgar studied him. "Six months. Wait… Senator Zenk. I thought that must be you."

"Zenk and Arthurs, the FBI assistant director, and it wasn't me personally, but—"

"Danny. Arthurs's death was classic Danny."

"Danny was working with Jackson and Cranford, but things went south so he—"

"Did what Danny does best. Go in alone and get lethal."

Simon nodded.

"So those men, they were the backers for the cartel?"

"And the pirates who took down the *Ridgeway*. But we knew they weren't the only ones. There was more money and someone with a tactical brain behind it all. Someone military."

"What the hell do they want? More than just money obviously."

"If we knew that, we'd have them. I've got a name but nothing concrete, no solid explanation except money, power, the usual."

"You're investigating this for the CIA?" Simon could tell Edgar was skeptical, almost as skeptical as Simon had been when Derrick had called. He chewed on his lip as he decided what and what not to say.

"Before I go any further, are you in?"

"In?" Edgar raised his brows.

"On the mission. We're going to find Admiral Kingsford and he's going to tell us the fucking truth."

Edgar's eyes widened. "Kingsford? Fucking Kingsford, decorated admiral who gave you a command, is the fucking military connection to this bunch of goatfucking bastards?"

"Yes. Well, I'm ninety-five percent certain. He sure as hell was the power behind the men who shot me a few days ago. But we need proof and we have to move quickly to get it. His fucking henchmen already know I'm investigating him, but they aren't sure how much I know and I have no idea who they think I'm really working for."

"'We' meaning Danny and you against a small army with resources you couldn't dream of? That kind of 'we'?"

"Me, Danny and Sport, Jackson, a few other resources you haven't met, and you if you'll join us. So will you?"

"Si—"

"We're going to bring them down. Every fucking one of them who has anything to do with this. Don't you want to be part of it?"

Simon saw it, the moment Edgar went from "fuck no, I don't do fieldwork anymore, you son of a bitch" to "I need to be a part of this." He was going to give in. Now Simon just had to tread carefully so he didn't fuck this up.

You know you'll lure him in. You always do.

I'm sick of manipulating people, especially my fucking friends.

But you're so damn good at it.

"Kingsford. My God, Si. How can you act so calm about all this? You're going to tell me everything," Edgar demanded. "And then I'll think about it."

Simon licked his lips and then, keeping his voice

low, said, "I need you."

Edgar held up a hand. "Don't."

Simon sank his teeth into his bottom lip and held Edgar's gaze. "Edgar, I do."

"Stop doing this right fucking now."

Simon wanted to, but he had to use every trick he knew to get Edgar involved, even if it ultimately fucked up what they had. If Edgar were with him, then he'd have a better chance making sure Edgar survived too. Kingsford's men wouldn't hesitate to hurt anyone and everyone connected with Simon.

"There a lake house called The Retreat. It's in Suffolk near yours. We need to do some recon there, see if we can find something to prove Kingsford's involved with the organization that allowed the attack on my ship."

"How did you find the house? You said Derrick sent you?"

"I was held nearby. Derrick sent me to investigate a group of mercenaries. Turns out they're Kingsford's personal army. I knew it was a trap. Derrick even gave me a hint that tells me he's being forced to go along with Kingsford's men at the CIA."

"Wait. I thought the CIA were the ones investigating this whole fucking operation—Zenk, Arthurs, all of it."

Simon shrugged. "It's always more complicated than that."

Edgar sighed. "I'm not even going to ask why you took the mission when you knew it was a trap."

"I needed intel and I got it." Simon hated the look in Edgar's eyes that said Edgar felt sorry for him.

"What do you need me for? You've got Danny and plenty of others."

"We need your lake house as a base, and we need someone who'll take care of us."

Edgar shook his head vehemently. "I'm not your fucking babysitter, Simon."

Anger surged through Si. He half rose from his chair and slammed his hands down on the table. "Edgar, did you hear me? Fucking Kingsford fucking sold us out. Us and our whole fucking crew. If I hadn't disobeyed—"

"Goddammit, sit down, Simon. I get it, okay. I want the man found, I'd like to wrap my hands around his fat throat and squeeze until his eyes pop, but… I can't be what you want me to be."

"You already are." Simon's voice cracked on those words. Oh God. This was it, the moment of total breakdown. His eyes stung and his side burned. Had he pulled out his stitches jumping up like he had? *Idiot. Focus on the pain. That's something you can handle.* The swirl of emotions threatened to pull him under. That would be what ended him.

***

"Look at me," Edgar ordered.

When Simon did, Edgar's stomach knotted. There were tears in his eyes. "What did your captors do to you, Si?"

Simon shook his head. "Nothing. Nothing worse than usual anyway."

"Then what…?"

"We're so close to finishing this, and I'm…"

"Scared."

Simon nodded.

Edgar knew Simon wouldn't admit that to anyone else, not even Danny. He also knew Simon wasn't scared of dying or of confronting the man. He was scared of who he would be when it ended. Edgar understood that without Simon having to say another word.

What the hell could Edgar do to comfort him? Tell Simon he was scared too. Tell Simon he loved him and he'd follow him anywhere. His pulse pounded in his ears. Simon, Danny, and Edgar were all crazy from what they'd been through, but if they really had a lead, if they truly were as close as Simon thought to putting an end to the group of men who had orchestrated all these horrors, how could he refuse to help them?

Edgar's phone rang, breaking in to his thoughts. He shook his head, trying to clear it enough to remember where he'd left the damn thing.

Finally, he saw it on the counter. "It's Laura."

Simon nodded and he answered. "Hello."

"Hi, I just wanted to check on you, see how things were going."

"They're better. But I'm going to be taking a leave of absence, and I'll need you to cover for me if people start asking questions."

Si had gone back to wolfing down his burger, but he froze when Edgar said he'd be taking leave. Edgar glared at him and Si's lips curled up in a knowing smile. The smug bastard always got what he wanted.

"So better but also worse?" Laura asked.

"Physically better. The situation is more complicated than I'd guessed."

"So the mild-mannered doc is being called in on

something that's 'complicated'?"

Edgar laughed despite the gravity of the situation. "Yes. I shouldn't be gone long, but the less you know, the better."

"Let me know you're okay when you can."

"I will. Thanks for everything. You've been a great friend."

"Oh God, this is your goodbye speech, isn't it? The one you give if you think you're not coming back."

Of course she'd know that. "I'm coming back."

"You're not confident in your words. I can tell."

"Okay, Ms. Psych Expert, that's enough. I'll do everything I can to be back soon."

"Fine, but no goodbye speeches. That's too unsettling."

Edgar nodded even though she couldn't see him. "Just hold down the fort for me."

"With those old dinosaurs you work with? That won't be hard."

"I'll text you when I get home," Edgar promised.

"Do that. And watch your back."

He ended the call. Simon was watching him, no longer the eager, smug man he'd been. He looked annoyed and… jealous? *Fucking A!* Laura was right, and Edgar was just pissed off enough to use that knowledge to his advantage. This time, he was going to be the manipulator and Simon wouldn't stand a chance.

"So you *are* doing the mission with us?" Simon asked.

Edgar snorted. "As if you doubted it."

Simon's cheeky grin faded, and Edgar's heart

skipped a beat as he saw the anguish in Si's eyes.

"I did," Si said. "This time I really did." His words were clearly heartfelt. He'd dropped the front he usually put up and that almost made Edgar relent in his plan. Maybe he shouldn't fuck with Si… No, the bastard had played him too many times. He deserved to be pushed to the edge.

"You told Danny to meet us at my lake house, didn't you?" Edgar asked.

Simon had the nerve to look incredulous. "Were you listening to me? You were in the kitchen the whole time."

"Afraid I actually snuck up on you?" Edgar snorted. "I didn't need to listen in. I just know how to read you."

Si shook his head. "You always did, better than anybody else."

Not better than Laura apparently. After nothing but a single short meeting, she'd noted Simon's jealousy. Edgar had never seen it, but now, thinking back, he could list at least a dozen times Simon had warned him off someone or straight up cock-blocked him. He almost grinned at the memories, because now he knew the reason behind it. Maybe he hadn't wanted to see it until now.

"So when will Danny show up?"

"Let me check." Simon pulled out his phone and typed a message. A few seconds later, it chimed. "Midday tomorrow. Hopefully Sport and Jackson will be there too."

Edgar nodded. "So that gives me tomorrow morning to gather what we need while you rest. How long do you—"

"I'm done resting."

"The fuck you are. You can use the laptop, but that's it. Packing, gathering supplies, all of that is on me."

Simon sat up straighter and his expression hardened. "We're going to split that up. I've got a list of what we need. You'll—"

"No. You're staying right here. In bed." Edgar refused to let himself get bulldozed by Simon in planning mode. There was a reason Simon had made captain younger than anyone since World War II. The man could convince even a bitter rival to follow his plans, no matter how half-baked or dangerous.

Simon scowled. Edgar was probably the only person he'd let challenge him like that. "I'm not fucking helpless."

"True, you never have been. But you need to be at full strength if you'll be poking around Kingsford's house tomorrow."

Simon sighed and leaned forward onto his hands. "I hope to God we can pull this off with so little time to prepare."

Fuck. If Si was worried this wouldn't work… "If Sport and Jackson are as good as you say, then yes." As much as he wanted to inject some sanity into this day, he knew as well as Si did that they had no choice. If Kingsford were culpable, they would bring him down hard. The man would never even see a jail cell.

Si took a deep breath, and when he looked up, some of his color had returned. "They are and there's a guy from Sport and Jackson's team, Reed Devereaux. He was their tech expert. We'll get

72

support from him too."

"Good. How many days should I tell my partners I'll be gone. Two?" Edgar asked.

Simon nodded. "You won't need more than that. If we're not back in forty-eight hours, we've failed."

"And in that case, I likely won't be coming back at all." Edgar knew the reality. Laura might not want to hear it, but he was realistic.

Simon nodded, but he looked unsettled. Edgar didn't think it was just the possibility of the mission going south. That was always there, every time they went into the field. Had Si expected Edgar to put up a fight and was disappointed not to get it? Maybe he was just pissed that he wasn't in a position to take charge. Si hated giving up any measure of control. He wasn't going to admit how weak he was.

And if Si thought giving up total control of the mission was difficult, he had more frustration coming. Edgar had every intention of making Si give up control once Edgar forced him to confess that he wanted more than friendship. Edgar wanted Simon on his knees. He wanted Simon to beg. The idea of fucking Si, of fucking any man, should seem strange, but it didn't. This was his best friend. Edgar had cared about him for years, making their relationship physical seemed natural now.

Edgar sat back down to finish his dinner. Simon's burger was long gone, as were the fries, and he was halfway through a fourth—or was it fifth?— doughnut. He'd always eaten like that. When they'd run their first black ops mission together, Si had told him that as long as he'd packed a snack and gun, he was ready for anything.

"Where the hell do you put all that?" Edgar gestured at Simon's plate.

Simon just shrugged and stuffed the rest of the doughnut in his mouth. When his tongue snaked out to lick the cream from his lips, Edgar stifled a groan, turning it into a cough. He didn't want to be patient, but he was going to stick to his plan. He needed to make Simon state exactly what he wanted from Edgar so he couldn't pretend Edgar had imagined it later.

CHAPTER SEVEN

Simon had finally fallen asleep around midnight after trying to insist he needed to stay awake and prep for the mission. Edgar hadn't had much luck sleeping between dreams and worrying about Si and what they were walking into.

When Simon came out of the bedroom the next morning looking absurdly hot in a pair of Edgar's sleep pants that he'd had to roll up, Edgar was sitting on the couch. Edgar loved that Simon had chosen to wear Edgar's clothes rather than the sweats Edgar had bought him. The TV was on, but Edgar had no idea what he was watching. He shut it off when Simon slowly lowered himself until he was seated next to Edgar.

"You feeling okay?" Edgar asked.

"Fine. Just stiff and sore. You shouldn't have let me sleep so long."

"I shouldn't be letting you leave today." Edgar picked up his phone. Simon was barely awake, but if he didn't move forward with his plan now, the morning would rush by and then it would be too late. Simon would be back in his world and they would have to focus on the mission.

"What did you think of Laura?"

Simon frowned. "She's bossy and opinionated but obviously cares for you." Edgar didn't miss the fact that Simon nearly choked on those last words.

"Should I ask her out?"

Simon sputtered. "What? No."

Edgar almost felt sorry for Simon. Almost. "The last time you were here, you complained that I had no social life. Laura's been helping with that. She's smart, beautiful, not the type to be clingy. So I was thinking…"

Simon frowned. "I just wanted you to do something other than work. I didn't mean you had to…"

"So by 'get a social life' you meant friends, not dating?"

Simon's cheeks turned an adorable shade of pink. Edgar didn't think he'd ever seen the man blush. If he pushed much harder, he was going to tip Simon over into anger. He wasn't sure he cared. He shifted position, bringing his leg up onto the couch and facing Simon.

"Why shouldn't I ask her out, Si?"

Simon studied his clasped hands. "She's… just not right for you."

"So who *would* be right for me?"

Simon opened his mouth, but no words came out.

"Is there someone you have in mind for me?" Edgar asked, moving closer.

"We should really think about getting the supplies for the mission." Simon leaned back so Edgar was no longer in kissing range.

"You really aren't going to tell me, are you?" He should give up the game and make his own confession, but doubt stopped him. What if he'd read Simon wrong, or worse, what if it was all a game—

the flirting, the looks? Simon was a keen manipulator; he always had been.

"Tell you what? Why she's wrong for you? I don't know. She just is, okay?" Simon scowled, but Edgar saw terror in his eyes.

If he took this any further, he risked ruining their friendship, risked Simon walking away after this mission and never coming back. But he couldn't stop himself. Doubt and uncertainty fled. "I think *I* know. I think she's wrong because *you're* the only one who's right for me."

Simon's eyes widened. He flailed as he tried to push himself up from the couch. Edgar straddled him so he couldn't get away without hurting them both. "Enough games, Si. It's time to tell me the fucking truth."

Simon's pupils were huge and Edgar could see the pulse beating at his throat. He had an urge to run his tongue over the fluttering skin to see if that made it go even faster.

Simon licked his lips. "What truth? I don't know what—"

"Don't you dare play me, Si. You owe me more respect than that."

"I'm not…" The words died and Si looked away. "Please don't make me do this. It will ruin everything."

"Will it?" Maybe Simon hated that he wanted Edgar. Maybe he hated Edgar as much as Edgar had tried to hate Si when he'd sent him away. "Tell me you don't want me, and I'll let you up."

The burner phone he'd gotten for Simon buzzed, rumbling across the table. Both men froze. Then slowly, Edgar stood and glanced at the phone's screen. "Danny. He always did have perfect timing."

Simon reached for the phone gingerly, like he was afraid it would bite him. Or maybe he thought Edgar would pin him again if he moved too fast.

***

Simon's hands were so sweaty, he came close to dropping the phone. "Hello."

"You sound strange," Danny said.

There was no way in hell Simon could have schooled his voice after that encounter with Edgar. *Fucking God.* "I'm fine."

"That's not a code I've forgotten, is it?"

Simon laughed, but it sounded brittle. "No. Seriously, just…" He glanced at Edgar, then stood and walked into the bedroom. Edgar would listen in anyway if he wanted to, but at least Simon could pretend it was more private. "Things are weird here."

"Of course they are. What did you expect when you went to him for help? Again."

"They're weirder than expected." If Danny only knew.

Danny snorted. "I'm assuming I should bring an arsenal for this job."

"That seems prudent." Simon was glad to be thinking about blowing things up rather than blowing Edgar.

"The rest of the guys are in. We'll all be there close to the appointed time. Thank you for not leaving me out this time. Never do that again." Danny's words had a hard edge.

"Maybe there won't be a next time."

"I'd love to think that, but we both know better.

78

There are always secrets under layers of secrets."

Simon sighed. "So fucking true."

"Watch your back on the drive. How are you, by the way?"

"Better but…"

"Not your best?" Danny asked.

"I'll do."

"I never doubted it."

Simon ended the call and then sank onto the bed. A shiver ran through him as he remembered the way Edgar had looked at him as he held him down on the couch, his hard thighs pressing into Simon's own. Simon wasn't sure if Edgar had been about to kiss him or about to punch him. Maybe both. Simon would've taken either. He deserved the latter but wanted the former. He'd dreamed about kissing Edgar, fucking him. But a relationship with him would be a mistake, especially before the mission ended. Completely ended, not just this phase. He needed his head in the game, not between Edgar's legs.

Who the fuck are you kidding? You think you're going to work beside him and not crave him like a junkie with the shakes? At least if you finally let him fuck you, take you, own you, then maybe, just maybe, you can think about something else when you're around him.

No, it shouldn't be like that. He's not just some trick from a bar.

How should it be? Full of roses and candlelight? You think that's what's going to go down between the two of you? You think he's going to ply you with seductive caresses? What the fuck?

Did he? Was he that much of a fool? Did he think somehow he'd end this shit with Kingsford and then *boom!* Simon would be a different person and Edgar wouldn't care about what he'd done or who he'd been for the past five years? That was never going to happen.

Not that Simon needed to worry about the future since the chance that he would survive taking out Kingsford and whoever else was involved was too slim to bank on. If one of his crew had to sacrifice himself, it would be him. He was determined on that point. They all had someone except Edgar, and Edgar had a life that didn't involve Si even if Simon had accused him otherwise. Besides, he helped people, put them together instead of tearing them apart. Si dealt in death, not life. A good number of the men he'd killed were scum, but some of them had just been in the wrong place or been forced to do something disgusting to save someone they cared about. Was he any better than those he hunted?

You hate it. The killing.

But I do it.

So does Edgar when he has to.

He'd killed men on the *Ridgeway*, three of their crew who'd apparently been planted by the terrorists and two of the fuckers who'd come to finish them off as the ship sank. Simon had lain there, bleeding out, with Edgar hovering over his dying body, picking off anyone who came near them. And then he'd been hit from behind. Simon had screamed. In his mind, the scream had gone on forever, echoing and echoing, coming back at him from the sea spray. Probably he'd passed out when he realized they were both going to die.

But Edgar had only been hit by a tranq gun, and the people who pulled them out were CIA, or so they said at the time. It hadn't really been a rescue, though. Simon didn't remember much of the next few days, but Edgar did. He'd never told Simon all the details. All Simon knew was that his heart had stopped. He'd been gone for over a minute before Edgar had brought him back. Then he'd "died" twice more and Edgar kept on saving him, the first time on the concrete floor of a cell and the next time in some kind of clinic that might or might not have been run by the CIA.

Simon had woken up in pain, confused, and demanding to see Edgar, but the men who held him there wouldn't let him. He didn't see Edgar again for months. Once they knew Simon would survive so they could resurrect him as an angel of death, they forced Edgar to go back to the States. Edgar had fought them until they'd tranq'd him again. He'd been discharged from the Navy and they'd told him not to search for Si if he valued his life.

Of course he hadn't listened. Eventually Edgar had made contact with Danny, but by then Simon was in deep, his soul sold to the CIA to earn a reprieve for the insubordination that had saved most of his crew. They'd known exactly how to coerce him, by threatening to go after Edgar and his other officers. They'd promised to court-martial them if he didn't cooperate. He'd had no choice. He'd become the CIA's slave.

He'd given up his freedom so Edgar could keep on healing people. Simon was too scarred to ever be fully healed, but Edgar had the chance to be the man he was meant to be. Simon had tried to stay away from him, but he couldn't. Edgar had helped him again and again until Simon and Danny had dragged him to the jungle in South America.

They'd failed to save Jackson and Sport's team or the villagers they'd hoped to protect. And they'd lost Martin, a green operative the CIA had sent in like a lamb to the slaughter. Their whole team had been taken prisoner and Martin had been killed to scare them into talking. Edgar lost his stomach for fieldwork that day, but at least he'd kept his sanity. Simon wasn't sure he'd made out as well himself.

Simon curled in a ball on the bed. He wanted what Edgar was offering, but he didn't deserve it.

***

Edgar hadn't heard anything but silence from the bedroom for several minutes, yet Simon remained there with the door closed. He was ignoring Edgar, refusing to acknowledge what had just happened—or rather not happened thanks to Danny.

Edgar had seen the lust glazing Si's gorgeous eyes. No way in hell was Edgar going on this mission without clearing things up between them. To do that he was going to have to push and Simon was going to have to make the first move. Simon was a master at twisting words, making things seem like more or less than what they were. Edgar wouldn't give him so much as a kiss on the cheek before Si told him exactly what he wanted. The chance that this was going to fuck them both up was approaching a hundred percent, but Edgar was going to ride it out until they forced it to work or it blew up in their face.

It had been almost a year since Edgar had told Si not to come to him for help anymore, but Edgar had known he'd made a mistake almost immediately. He'd considered tracking him down and now he knew he should have. He'd let Si run toward death like he courted it. Si had lost his sense of self-preservation, and like it or not, Edgar had to help him get it back.

If Simon had really found the man who sank the *Ridgeway*, could Edgar help him heal or was it too late? Should he have done something more drastic before now? What could he have done? Si was so fucking stubborn, so persistent in what he believed. But that stubbornness had saved Edgar's life more than once.

Memories flashed. The jungle. A prison cell deep in the ground. The interrogation room, walls splattered with blood. The air filled with pain and fear. Yelling. The man who'd taken them pulling a gun. Edgar didn't think it was a real threat. The man had always let his lackeys do the dirty work before, but not this time,

"I've had enough." He raised his weapon. Edgar tensed. The guards moved back, as afraid of him as Edgar was. Simon glanced at Edgar and gave a signal. This was their chance, four against three and only one was paying attention. But before they could make a move, the man shot Martin three times in the chest. Bang. Bang. Bang. *Martin's eyes went wide and he sank to his knees, hands coming to his chest as if he could staunch the bleeding. "Fuck!" That was his last word.*

Simon and Danny leapt into action. Simon took the leader's gun and ended him. Danny took out both

guards, but Edgar crouched by Martin unable to do a damn thing but try to save him when he knew Martin was already dead. Blood was everywhere. Someone tugged on his arm. Simon.

"Come on. We've got to go."

"I can't leave him. He's... I've got to help."

Danny and Simon manhandled Edgar out of there with Si's hand over his mouth to cover his protests.

He'd lost it completely. He might have ruined the escape for all of them, gotten all of them killed, but he'd never left anyone behind.

Edgar shook his head to clear it. Did Simon really trust him to go back in the field? Did he think Edgar was anything but a liability? If there was a chance they could take out this organization, Edgar was going in with them. But he needed details. He needed Simon to let him in all the way. Edgar smiled at the unintentional innuendo. He wasn't sure if that kind of going in would make the mission easier or harder—probably both.

Simon obviously didn't want to talk anymore, but fuck that. Edgar wouldn't push for a declaration about the two of them, but he would demand answers. How had Simon found out about Kingsford? Who was really pulling the strings on this mission? He wasn't going in as blind as he'd been in the jungle. He'd thought they were on a scouting mission. Simon swore he hadn't known the details until they were already there. Maybe that was true, but Edgar had never truly believed him.

He poured coffee for himself and Simon. When he reached the bedroom, he didn't knock. It was his fucking house, after all. What he saw when he opened the door made him freeze. Simon was curled on his side on the bed, his body shaking with sobs. *Fucking hell.*

Si didn't move, but he had to know Edgar was there. Edgar put the drinks on the nightstand and stretched out on the bed next to him. Simon was so still, Edgar didn't even think he was breathing. Edgar spooned him, but he kept his touch comforting rather than sexual. "I'm right here. I can protect you, Simon, at least for now."

Simon swiped at his eyes, but he didn't say anything. He also didn't move away. Edgar held him until he fell asleep. Then he stood, gulped down his coffee, and went to sort out the gear they'd need. He didn't like leaving Si on his own in this state. Should he call Laura? She was stronger than she looked, but she was no match for the kind of men Si was mixed up with. Having her stand guard over Simon was more of a risk than he should take. But in the end, he called her anyway.

CHAPTER EIGHT

Simon awoke drenched in sweat as a familiar nightmare faded. Something felt off. The apartment was too still. He remained frozen, not wanting to give away his alertness. When he'd listened long enough to feel confident no one was in the room with him, he picked up the gun Edgar had left him and moved slowly toward the bedroom door.

It was open just a crack. He waited, listening, letting all his senses take in the apartment. He heard a creak, like someone shifting in a chair. It wasn't Edgar. He couldn't say how he was certain of that, but he was. He moved down the hall, keeping close to the wall. He could see the kitchen. No one was there. Heart pounding, he turned to the living room, weapon out.

Laura sucked in her breath and held up her hands. "It's me."

Simon surveyed the rest of the room and then lowered his weapon. "Where's Edgar?"

"Running errands that probably have to do with whatever is keeping him out of the office next week."

Simon nodded. "And you're my babysitter?"

"That's not how Edgar put it."

"Well, however he put it, you can go. The only reason I'd need help would be if a few… 'friends' caught up to me. If that happens, you need to be far away from here."

She gave him a bright smile, much too knowing for his taste. "Edgar told me you'd be an ass if you woke up."

"I'm not a safe person to be around."

"You're hurt, physically and emotionally. And you're scared, but you'll never admit it. You're used to getting your way."

Simon rolled his eyes. "God, I hate shrinks."

"You could use one, though."

"No, I could use a drink and a couple of miracles." Simon headed toward the kitchen. It was time for some of the Bushmills he'd not been able to appreciate the day before.

"You care for him, don't you?"

"He saved my life more than once and I don't mean that metaphorically. So yeah, I care for him. He's one of the very few people I trust."

Laura smiled.

Simon knew the wheels were turning, analyzing his relationship with Edgar. "Don't go there. No one who hasn't been through the shit we have could possibly understand how we feel about each other."

She nodded. "I see. So in other words, it's complicated. Is that it?"

Simon resisted the urge to flip her off. She was Edgar's friend, after all. He poured his drink. Took a sip. Searched for a snack. Opened a container of mixed nuts, ate a handful. More whiskey. The silence was starting to get to him. "Of course I fucking care," he muttered.

Laura was smiling at him again.

"Quit judging me. You don't get it. You don't

understand what I've put him through." Wait. How the fuck did she have him talking? He was playing right in to her hands.

"I'd be happy to listen if you'd like me to."

Simon shook his head. "I'd like you to go."

"Are you always this charming?"

He laughed. "Actually, I'm the one they send to charm, seduce, convince a target to do exactly what they want. No one can say no to me."

She studied him for a few seconds, then nodded. "I can see that. You just hate being seduced yourself."

"Ha! You're not my type and I thought you and Edgar had something going on."

Laura laughed and shook her head. "Edgar and I slept together a few times when we first met. Then we realized we made much better friends than lovers. We were both hung up on someone else."

Simon reacted with surprise before he could stop himself.

Who the hell is Edgar hung up on? Me? No fucking way!

Then why did he lie to you about asking her out?
Because he's an ass.

He pinned you down last night, literally.

"So you're just friends?"

"Yes. I lost my husband a little more than a year ago, and I'm not ready to move on yet."

"I'm sorry." Simon meant that sincerely. He could see the pain in her expression. The thought of losing Edgar made him ill.

"Thank you."

"And Edgar?"

"What about him?" Laura asked, eyes focused on

him like a hawk studying its prey.

"Who was he—never mind." What was he thinking? He didn't want to ask her that. "You really can go. I'm not helpless, no matter what Edgar may have told you."

"You're recuperating from a gunshot wound. Accepting some help is hardly out of line." At least she wasn't pushing for him to restate his question.

"I've had worse."

"I've heard that too."

"Just how much has Edgar told you about me?" Simon didn't like the thought of them analyzing him together. In fact, it made him want to start a fight with Edgar as soon as he got home. A rough, sweaty fight that would... Fucking hell, now he was starting to get hard.

"He's told me very little actually."

Simon wasn't sure whether he liked that answer or not.

"I don't need a lot to go on."

"Yeah, he mentioned you were some kind of psych superstar."

She smiled. "I've made a name for myself in my field."

"So have I," Simon responded.

"And your field is?"

"That's classified, ma'am."

The overly pleased expression on her face made Simon nervous.

"So Edgar puts up with you analyzing him?" Simon asked. "I have a hard time imagining that."

"I've actually never given him advice until yesterday."

"And what did you say?"

She raised her brows. "You have to know I'm not going to tell you that."

Simon gave her his patented softening-up smile. "You can't blame me for trying."

"Very nice. Edgar warned me you were a master at diversion and manipulation."

Simon pulled out his weapon when he heard someone approaching the door. Laura watched him, not saying a word. He positioned himself to protect her if that someone wasn't Edgar, though by the cadence of the steps, Simon was sure it was. A key went into the lock and it clicked open. Then the doorknob turned and Edgar called out, "Simon, it's all clear out here. Put down your weapon."

Simon did as asked and Edgar stepped into the apartment.

Laura looked back and forth between the two of them. "How did you know he was there?" she asked Edgar.

"Instincts. And years together."

Laura frowned. "But he was soundly sleeping when you left."

"I knew he'd be awake by now, and he hears everything."

"When you haven't drugged me," Simon added.

"Yes, there's an exception to everything." The bastard still showed no remorse for what he'd done.

"Very interesting," Laura said, obviously reading a hell of a lot into their interaction. Simon didn't want to think about the tales she was spinning in her head. It didn't matter, though. He'd heard how fucked-up he was from numerous professionals and he didn't care. He got the job done and what he had or didn't have with Edgar was no one's fucking business, even if Laura was Edgar's friend.

"Thank you," Edgar said. "I hope he wasn't too much of a pain in the ass."

"We got along just fine." She gave Simon a knowing look.

"I'm right here and I'm an adult. A very capable adult."

Edgar gave Simon a slow once-over that had his cock perking up. The little bastard. "Yes, you certainly are."

What was Edgar playing at?

"I've got more bags in the car. Walk down with me?" Edgar asked Laura.

More cozy time? What the fuck? She'd said they weren't dating, that they'd tried and it hadn't worked. Maybe Edgar—the lying bastard—wanted to grill her about Simon.

***

"So did you work up a case study?" Edgar asked.

Laura laughed. "He was only awake for ten minutes before you got home."

"Two minutes would have been enough for you."

"I think you're overestimating my skills."

Edgar raised his brows and studied her until she relented.

"He's hurting and scared. Nothing I said earlier has changed. He's in love with you, and he won't admit it. He thinks it's his job to protect everyone, and he doesn't know how to accept your concern for him."

"Is that *it*?" Edgar asked.

"Hardly. Simon could provide me with enough material for an entire book."

How did she figure all that out so quickly? Of course Edgar couldn't be sure she was right. Maybe she was seeing what she wanted to see. "If you had access to the men I'll be spending the weekend with, you could write a whole series."

"No doubt. Watch your back this weekend." Laura opened her car door and set her purse inside.

"I will."

"And tell Simon how you feel before you go."

"I tried to tell him, but I don't think he was listening." He'd actually tried to make Simon tell him, but it amounted to the same thing.

"He is going to fight this as hard as he can," Laura said as she settled into the driver's seat.

"Why?"

"Fear that he'll screw up, that he's damaged, that you're too good for him."

Edgar shook his head. "No fucking way." Edgar couldn't see Simon thinking that way. He was too fucking arrogant.

"Everything he does is a cover. He's buried his real self so deep it will take months of peeling off layers to get to him. You're going to have to be patient."

"I've waited years. I can be patient now." *If we live that long.* Edgar closed Laura's car door for her and waved goodbye.

When he stepped back into the apartment. Simon was eating a bowl of Cocoa Puffs, which Edgar had bought just for him. How was it that one of the most dangerous men in America ate like a four-year-old?

Simon didn't say anything, but Edgar could feel Simon's eyes on him as he unloaded the things he'd bought, stuffing some of them into a duffel and others, like the food, into a cooler or carrier bags.

The only sounds in the room were the rustling bags and Simon's crunching. Simon poured himself a second bowl, and by the time Edgar was done packing the supplies, he was reaching for the box again. If Edgar hadn't already admitted it to himself, finding Simon's greed for sugar-coated sugar balls adorable would have warned him he was head over heels for Simon.

Don't leave without telling him. Time to try again because Laura was right. He and Simon couldn't go into this mission without clearing things between them.

He sat down at the table and started fiddling with his phone.

"What are you doing?" Simon asked just as Edgar had predicted he would. He was too curious for his own good, especially when it came to "his crew," whether they were on a ship any longer or not.

"Calling Laura."

"Why? Did you forget to tell her something?"

"I thought it would be helpful if she brought more sedative so I can knock you out again."

Simon flipped him off.

"Did you take any pain pills?"

"No. I can't. I'm not letting you—or Laura or whoever you send to babysit me next—get killed because I'm high."

Edgar held up a hand. "Fine." He wished Simon would give himself that comfort for the few hours they had before heading to the lake house, but that was not the argument he wanted to have.

"So why are you really calling her?"

"If I live through this weekend, I want to make some changes. I should have done it while she was here, but I'm going to ask her out now."

Simon's gaze hardened. "She told me that you'd fucked each other and then decided things didn't work between you."

"Did she now?" Edgar refused to let Si rattle him. Of course he'd gotten Laura to talk about her personal life when no one else could.

"Why did you lie to me?"

"Lie to you?" *Play innocent.*

"About asking her out?"

"I didn't. She's had more time to mourn her husband now. I thought we could try again."

"No." Simon's voice was hard, his body tense. He had the look of hyperfocus he got during battle.

Edgar couldn't stop his lip quirking up in a half smile. Simon was playing right along. Most people who knew Simon backed off when he shifted into defensive mode, but not Edgar. In fact, he courted it, because Si was less likely to manipulate when he was angry. "Why not?"

Simon glared at him as if trying to bend Edgar to his will with his gaze.

Edgar shrugged, pretending he didn't know Simon was ready to snap. "If you can't give me a good reason, I'm calling." He scrolled through the contacts, found Laura's name, and held up the screen so Simon could see.

When Simon said nothing, Edgar moved his

finger to the Call icon.

Despite his injury, Simon was out of his seat in a flash. He knocked the phone from Edgar's hand.

Edgar shoved him, catching him off guard. Then he dove for the phone, but it slid across the tile.

Simon grabbed Edgar, rolling him, slamming his back against the floor, and knocking the breath out of him. Simon got his feet under him then, but Edgar kicked out, hitting his ankle and bringing him down again.

Edgar took advantage of Simon's fall to go on the offensive. He grabbed Si's shoulders and shoved him to the floor. Simon hit hard and groaned. Edgar raised off him, mindful of his wound. Simon took the opportunity to try and land a fist in Edgar's gut, but Edgar caught his arms and pinned them over his head.

Had Simon let him do that? He'd never beaten Simon in hand-to-hand combat. Si's injury might have made him slower, but not by much. Edgar wasn't going to complain, though. Simon giving in was exactly what he wanted.

He stretched out on top of Simon, bringing their bodies into full contact. He'd seen Simon naked countless times, and he'd fought with him, either sparring or when they were pissed off and drunk, but now that he'd admitted what he felt for Si, all those muscles and valleys, the hard and soft spots under him, felt very different. This wasn't two friends wrestling or letting off steam. Edgar's cock responded to Simon's halfhearted struggle—no way did he believe Simon was incapable of throwing him off, especially not now that Edgar was distracted by feelings he'd never had for another man.

Simon glared at him. Edgar saw anger in his eyes but also fear and something else, something softer than either of those. Edgar smiled and Simon bucked under him, getting more serious about freeing himself.

Edgar thrust against Si, using his hips to push Simon back to the floor and letting Simon feel exactly what all the friction between them was doing to him.

Simon's eyes widened and Edgar chuckled. "If you didn't want this, you'd have gotten free."

Simon shook his head. "I'm injured, as you keep reminding me."

"Bullshit. There's not been a moment since you walked through that door half-dead that you couldn't have ultimately gotten the best of me."

"I'm not sure about that." Simon closed his eyes and turned his head.

Edgar rocked his hips against Si, rubbing his erection along Simon's growing one. The shudder that went through Si made Edgar's cock harden even more.

"Look at me," Edgar demanded.

Simon ignored him, but when Edgar ground against him again, Simon finally opened his eyes. Edgar had never seen him look that uncertain before.

"Wh-what's happening here?" Simon asked.

Edgar grinned. "I really thought you had more experience than that."

"But… But you…" Simon licked his lips, and Edgar couldn't help staring at his mouth.

Kiss him.

Not yet.

"I've wanted you for a long time, but I ignored it.

Then when I couldn't ignore it anymore, I tried to make it go away, but it didn't. And now… I'm tired of fighting and tired of you running away."

"Please don't ask Laura out." Simon held Edgar's gaze with his beautiful eyes. Edgar knew he was scared, because Edgar sure as hell was.

"Why?"

"Because I… Fuck, why are you doing this?"

"I'm not doing anything," Edgar insisted. And it was true. The chemistry between them wasn't his doing. He doubted it was Simon's either. He'd never believed in fate, but whatever the hell had brought them together was a force stronger than either of them and it was something they couldn't fight.

"Simon, tell me."

Simon opened his eyes again and scowled at Edgar. "Because you're mine."

That was exactly what he'd wanted to hear. "Am I now?"

Simon nodded, looking terrified. Did he really think Edgar would reject him now? Edgar rocked his hips again, grinding down harder this time.

Simon sucked in his breath.

"Like that, do you?"

"Edgar, don't tease me."

"I can't believe that just came out of your mouth, after all the times you've toyed with me, strung me along—"

"Not about this. I'd never…" He looked so fucking adorable, all wide-eyed and off his game.

"You know what?" Edgar asked.

"What?"

"I think you're wrong."

Simon looked away, his body going tense. "About what?"

"I think that actually, *you're* mine." Before Simon could react, Edgar crushed Simon's lips under his.

CHAPTER NINE

Simon's head spun as Edgar pulled back from kissing him. He couldn't believe this was happening, but if it was a dream, it was the best one he'd had in a long time. And it goddamn well better not end in death and horror. He thrust back against Edgar, squirming under him, fighting to get loose, not because he wanted to get away, but because he needed the freedom to touch Edgar. He'd jerked off countless time thinking about running his hands over Edgar's body and how fucking good Edgar's cock would feel ramming his ass. "Fuck," he gasped as Edgar shifted his attention to Simon's neck, kissing and nibbling. "Is this real?"

Edgar rubbed his hard cock against Si's. "That's sure as hell not pretend."

Fuck no, it wasn't. Simon sucked in his breath. He'd seen Edgar's cock before. They'd showered together, shared a bed, changed in all kinds of conditions, but he didn't think he'd ever seen him fully hard, and holy fuck he felt good. Big, thick, solid. And ready to fuck Simon. "Have you been hiding this from me?"

Edgar frowned. "Hiding what?"

"Being gay?"

"I'm not gay. I… I guess I'm bi, but I've never been with a man before."

"And you're okay with—" Simon arched up, dragging his now hard cock along Edgar's. Jesus, that felt good. "—this."

Edgar nodded. "It's you. And it feels fucking good."

Simon grinned, trying to look more confident than he felt. "Of course it does."

Edgar glared. "Don't."

"Don't what?" Simon started to feel awkward pinned under Edgar, a man he'd wanted for years. A man he'd been certain was straight and out of reach. He had to get things back under his control.

"Pretend. Put on a front. I want *you*, Si, not the man you pretend to be."

How was he going to be with someone who could see through him? That was why he never slept with friends. Danny was gorgeous, and so many times it would have been convenient as hell for them to blow off steam together. But he'd never gone there. "It's sex, Edgar. Wouldn't you rather me be at my most seductive?"

For just a second, hurt flashed in Edgar's gaze before anger replaced it. "You really think that's all this will be?"

"It… No." Edgar had loosened his grip so Simon pushed against his hands and flipped them easily.

"You think you're going to top me?" Edgar asked.

Simon looked into his eyes. They were darker than usual, and he could see Edgar's desire there. Edgar wasn't faking this. He really fucking wanted Simon.

This is a disaster. "I'm not going to be on top or

anywhere else because this isn't going to happen."
But Jesus, how I wish it could.

"Si, you just told me—"

"I shouldn't have. We shouldn't be together. But no one's good enough for you, okay?"

"Simon." The word came out as a growl.

It didn't matter that Edgar was pinned under him now. Simon felt as trapped as he had before. "This can't happen."

"Tell me why."

"Because being with you will distract me. And I can't afford that. I have to be—"

Edgar arched a brow and gave Simon his stop-bullshitting-me look. "Si, I've heard the all-sacrificing leader speech enough times that I could give it for you in my sleep. A few seconds ago, you were honest. You were my Simon, not an operative, not a man charming his way into an organization he intended to bring down all by himself—"

"I've never brought down an entire…" But that wasn't the point, was it? Edgar didn't care about that. He cared about something Simon couldn't give him.

Edgar watched him. "I know your secrets, Si. You can't hide from me."

"What if this—?"

"What if it changes everything? What if we fuck up what we have? I don't know. I don't have all the answers. But I'm tired of letting fear stop me from doing this." He cupped Simon's face and pulled him down.

When their lips met, Simon sighed into his mouth. Edgar kissing him was fucking perfect, like he'd been born to kiss Simon. Edgar teased his lower lip with his tongue, then pushed inside, all the time holding Simon firmly, making him understand Edgar wasn't going anywhere without a fight. Edgar was in control, and Simon—who always wanted to run things, whose leadership skills were still being taught at Officer Candidate School though the men were told he'd died on the *Ridgeway*—loved it.

Edgar nibbled his jaw. And Simon whimpered. *Fuck!* How did Edgar manage to drag such sounds out of him?

"I don't," Simon protested when Edgar pulled back, but he couldn't get out any more words before Edgar took possession of mouth again.

"Don't what?" Edgar asked a few seconds later.

"Think I'm going to be on top."

"Damn right you're not, and it's not because I'm scared to have something up my ass. It's because that's what you need. Me inside you. You getting fucked."

Edgar licked the edge of Simon's ear and Simon whimpered again. Edgar chuckled, his warm breath tickling Simon. "How did you…?"

"Because if it wasn't, you'd already have me on my hands and knees."

"No, this is crazy. We really—"

"Simon, this is happening. I'm going to fuck you before we leave and risk our lives together. I will not let this start all over again until I know what you sound like as you come with my cock buried in you."

"Fucking hell, Edgar. Where did you learn to talk like that?"

"*You're* asking someone else about their dirty mouth?"

Silvia Violet

"I've never said anything like that to you."
Simon only wished he had.

"No, just to men and women you seduced in
front of me."

He'd been listening? Simon had thought he'd
have been too busy with his own partners or sleeping.
"But that was… I never sounded as hot as you doing
it."

"Trust me, you did." Edgar's lascivious smile
sent heat racing through Simon.

"Wait, how long have you wanted this? Me?"
"Years?"

"But I thought…" How the hell had he not
known?

Edgar sighed. "I let you think it because I was
scared."

"So now you're not?"

"Now I'm tired. Tired of fighting, tired of
watching you leave, tired of pretending my career is
enough."

"Fuck, Edgar. What are you saying? You really
don't just want to fuck and get this out of our
systems, do you?" Simon had rarely been as scared as
he was right then.

Edgar flipped them again, slamming Simon's
wrists to the floor. "No, I do not want to 'get this out
of my system'. If years of you acting like an arrogant
ass, years of you only calling on me whenever it was
convenient or whenever you needed to be put back
together hasn't gotten you out of my system, then
fucking you sure as hell isn't going to do it either. Si,
this is about more than sex. You goddamn well know
it and you're going to say so before we go any

further."

"Wh-what?"

You love him. You know you do.

"Simon, you're trying my patience almost as much as when you asked me to leave you to fucking die on the *Ridgeway*."

Simon couldn't have answered if he'd wanted to. His mouth had gone completely dry. This couldn't be happening. He should never have run to Edgar. This wasn't the time for Edgar to have realized what Simon had always known, that no one else was ever going to be right for him.

It's never going to be the right time.

"Say it, Simon."

"I… I can't."

"I'll wait. All day if I have to. I'll make us late to meet Danny." The tightness of his jaw signaled how serious he was.

"This mission isn't just about us. The men behind the attacks like one on our ship haven't stopped. We set them back six months ago, but there are plans in motion that they are going to ruin more lives, kill more operatives, more sailors. We have to stop them." Simon realized his voice was rising. He was starting to sound hysterical.

Edgar sat up and pulled Simon into his lap. "We will. But we can't focus on a mission, no matter how important, unless we settle things here." He pushed down the too-large sleep pants Simon had borrowed until he'd freed Simon's cock. Simon gasped at his touch, and when Edgar started stoking his cock, Simon couldn't stay still. If Edgar kept that up, Simon was going to come in seconds like a fucking teenager.

"Edgar, what the fuck are you doing?"

"I'm jerking you off, dear. I really thought you were more experienced than this."

"Edgar. You..." He was too good. He knew exactly how Simon wanted to be touched. "Fuck! How do you know just what I—"

"I do this to myself too, you know. You don't have to be gay to know how to stroke a fucking cock."

It was more than that, though. It was like they'd been fucking for months, years, like he could read Simon's fucking mind.

"You're about to come, aren't you?" Simon hated the smugness of Edgar's tone.

"No."

"Yes, you are. And you're going to tell me what I want to hear before you do."

Simon shook his head. "I can't."

"Then I'll have to stop." Edgar slowed his strokes until his hand was barely moving.

"No, please." Simon had been with a lot of men and women in his life and he'd done some kinky shit along with the usual sucking and fucking. How was it that this simple hand job from a man who'd never even held another man's dick before was the most amazing thing he'd ever experienced?

"Tell me how you feel, Simon."

"Can't." He barely pushed the word out. His cock was so hard. All it would take for him to come was just a few strokes, just a little more pressure.

He bucked, trying to force his cock through Edgar's fist.

"No you don't." Edgar squeezed the base of

Simon's dick, preventing him from coming.

"Fuck! I was so close." Simon wanted to scream, but not just from sexual frustration. Edgar was offering Simon everything he wanted, but if Edgar realized how fucked up he really was, he wouldn't want him anymore.

"Please!" Simon begged.

"Tell me what you need."

"I need to fucking come."

Edgar growled. "Simon."

"Goddammit, Edgar!"

Edgar started jacking him again. "You like my hand around your dick, don't you?"

"Y-yes. I just never thought you…"

"Neither did I, but I like it too, the heft of it, the way you react, how you're ready to come from me touching you." He rubbed his thumb over Simon's slit, smearing a drop of precum around.

"I don't…" Edgar thumbed his slit again and Simon lost the ability to form a sentence.

"Talk to me, Simon." Edgar returned to slow, lazy strokes of Simon's shaft.

"Why can't we just have fun with each other?" Simon asked.

"Because I want you all to myself, and you must feel the same way since you stopped me from pursuing Laura."

Simon's chest tightened. He didn't want Edgar with anyone else. Simon loved him, but he couldn't possibly… "Please, don't push me." He forced himself to close his eyes so he couldn't see Edgar's hand looking so right on his cock.

***

Edgar hated the pain on Simon's face. He knew Laura was right, that Simon loved him. He wanted him to say it, but he was being unfair by not saying it himself. If he pushed Simon more now, he'd probably fuck up the slim chance they had of making this work.

Maybe what they both needed was just to get off together. Hell, it was a start, and he fucking loved the feel of Simon's cock in his hand. It was like touching himself and yet not. He wanted to feel Si against him, so he undid his own pants and lined their cocks up so he could stroke them both.

"Edgar!" Simon gasped, dropping his head back. "That feels so fucking good."

"Enjoy it, okay? Don't worry about anything else."

Simon nodded, his blue eyes were bright, and he'd sunk his teeth into his lower lip like he was holding back something. Sounds. Words. Emotions.

When Edgar stroked them both, Simon groaned and worked his hips, trying to get more. "I love this, Simon, the feel of your cock against mine. It's strange and yet so right, so much better without all that fabric between us." Simon groaned and laid his hand over Edgar's. "I love how responsive you are. I want to see you come. God, Si, I've waited so long for this."

He worked them faster, harder. In no time he was riding the edge, determined to hold back until Simon came.

Simon thrust into his hand, working his cock along Edgar's. "Fuck. I'm close. Edgar! Fuck!"

"Come, Simon. I want to watch."

"Oh my fucking God!" Cum shot from Si's cock,

coating Edgar's hand, spilling onto his dick. Edgar fucking loved it. No way in hell was once going to be enough.

Simon pushed Edgar's hand away and started stroking Edgar himself. "I love you, Edgar. I've fucking loved you for years."

Oh my fuck. He'd said more than Edgar dreamed he would. Edgar made a strangled sound, the words he wanted to say stolen by an orgasm so strong he literally saw stars. Simon kept working him until he'd drained Edgar dry.

"Oh my God that... I love you too."

"Are you telling me we could've been doing that for years?"

Edgar shook his head. "I didn't realize how I felt until the jungle."

Simon's eyes widened in surprise. "Why then?"

Edgar wasn't sure how to explain it. He didn't remember the trek through the jungle to the extraction point, but he did remember Simon comforting him in the helo: stroking his hair, kissing his head, telling him he would be okay. For once, Simon was the one putting Edgar back together. He'd slumped against Si and drawn from his warmth, from what he suddenly realized was love. The more Simon had held him, the more warmth turned to wanting. It had scared him.

Later he'd thought it was just the stress of the situation, but from that time on, he saw Si differently. He was aware of him physically and aware that he wanted to spend the rest of his life with Simon, not as warriors on the same team, but as lovers.

Simon studied him, still breathing hard. "Wait, is that why you refused to go into the field afterward?"

"No, I didn't trust myself in the field anymore just like I said."

"You're lying," Simon said.

He was. He'd run from what he felt but probably not for the reasons Simon thought.

"Fine. I was fucking scared, okay? Scared I'd tell you how I felt and you'd laugh at me. Scared of fucking up our friendship or having you die as soon as we got together. I couldn't stand watching you take unnecessary risks again and again."

"And now?"

"Hiding didn't help," Edgar said.

"Running didn't either."

They stared at each other, and as Edgar watched Simon, his too-beautiful-to-be-real eyes, his perfect hair, lips that quirked up in an I-can-have-anything-I-want smile. Edgar's cock started to harden again. He needed Simon because Simon made him whole, made him forget the things that plagued him at night. Si needed him too.

Simon moved off Edgar and stood. Edgar's chest tightened. If Simon dismissed this, if he shrugged off what had just happened between them, Edgar wasn't sure how he would handle it.

Simon held out his hand and smiled, not the look he used to bend everyone to his will, the smile he gave Edgar when he thought no one was looking. "So what do we do now?"

"I don't fucking care. If we have today. If we have a year. If we have until we're a hundred. I want you."

Simon wrapped a hand around the back of Edgar's neck and kissed him, not gently—this wasn't a sweet confession of love—but hard and demanding. Simon was claiming him and Edgar had every intention of doing some claiming of his own.

He pushed the loose pants down Simon's legs, needing to touch skin. Fucking hell, Simon's ass felt good, solid, tight muscle. He used his grip to haul Simon against him. Simon must have felt that same need to touch, because he shoved Edgar's shirt up and dug his fingers into Edgar's back. Then he slid one hand around to caress his abdomen. Moving higher, he brushed his thumb over Edgar's nipple, causing him to groan. Simon's twisted the nub hard, and Edgar sank his teeth into Simon's lip in retaliation. Then he jerked Simon's head to the side and sucked at his neck, not giving a fuck who would see the mark if he left one.

"Edgar!" Simon cried.

"Mine. You're mine."

"You're going to fuck me." Simon reached between them and pressed his hand to Edgar's cock. "Right fucking now." He tried to get Edgar's jeans off, cursing when the zipper stuck.

Edgar forced himself to pull away. "We're doing this in bed."

Simon frowned. "I'm not sure my legs work. I think you broke me."

Edgar laughed as he picked Simon up. They were going to bed no matter how they had to get there. Edgar made sure the security system was on as they passed the control box. They didn't need someone surprising them, but no matter how foolish they were to let themselves get distracted like this, Edgar wasn't going to stop.

CHAPTER TEN

Simon bounced when he hit the bed. He loved Edgar going all caveman on him. "You got lube? Condoms?"

Edgar smiled. "I said I was getting all the supplies for the trip, didn't I?"

He tossed lube and a large box of condoms on the bed. "Fucking hell," Simon said, opening the box. "Confident, aren't you?"

"Yes."

Simon stopped opening the condom and watched as Edgar kicked off his jeans and yanked off his shirt. The workout Edgar had done the night before was obviously part of his regular routine. His chest was perfection: hard muscle, dark hair. And his thighs, Simon wanted to lick them, bite them, squeeze them while sucking Edgar's cock. There were so many things he wanted to do with Edgar, some of which Edgar might never have considered, but right then, all he cared about was Edgar inside him.

"Need you." The words came out breathy and desperate. Simon should have been ashamed of feeling so weak, but with Edgar he didn't care.

"Have you ever slept with anyone who actually knew *you* instead of just your façade?"

Simon didn't want to think about how well Edgar knew him. "I…"

"I'll take that as a no."

"Fuck, Edgar."

"Yes, I'm going to fuck *you*, Simon. Not the manipulative bastard you usually are."

Those words terrified Simon. Could he let go like that with Edgar? His hand shook as he grabbed the lube. He wasn't going to back out now.

He slicked a few of his fingers. Edgar watched, eyes filled with lust as Simon lay back and lifted his legs, then pushed two fingers in at once.

"Mmmm," he moaned. "Feels good, but I don't usually need a slow start like this. I don't mind some pain, but you'll find it easier to fuck a man for the first time if I'm nicely stretched out for you."

He worked his fingers in and out and added a third. Edgar's mouth hung open and his gaze never left Simon's ass.

"Is this vulnerable enough for you?" Simon asked. "I'm open for you in every way."

Edgar growled as he grabbed Simon's hand and pushed it out of the way. "Put your arms over your head and don't fucking move."

"Jesus!" When Edgar acted all dominant like that, he could have anything he wanted from Simon, even his fucking soul.

"I'm going to fuck you so hard you'll never consider running from me again."

"Please!" Simon hated how desperate he sounded, but he couldn't help it. Edgar had stripped away all his defenses.

Edgar picked up the condom Simon had been trying to open and ripped the package viciously. Simon squeezed the pillow under his head so hard he wondered why it didn't rip. He wanted to touch Edgar, to flip them over so he could ride him. He wanted control, but he fought those needs because what he really wanted was for Edgar to tell him what to do.

"You're not in charge here, Simon," Edgar said as he slicked his cock.

Simon sucked in his breath. How did Edgar know what he was thinking? "Did you just read my fucking mind?"

"I know you, Si. And I know what you need."

Simon squirmed, ready to beg Edgar to hurry the hell up. "I know what you need too. You need to claim me, make me surrender so I don't run. After all the hell I've given you, you want to put me in my place."

"Fuck yes, I do."

"Then do it already." Simon turned over, moving onto his hands and knees and sticking out his ass. "Because for once I want to be taken down a notch. I want to give in. To let you win, to be fucking owned."

Edgar made no attempt to be gentle. He brushed the tip of his cock over Simon's hole and then pushed in.

Simon gasped. "Fuck, that's—"

He choked on the rest of his words as Edgar thrust harder, balls slapping against Simon's ass. "Jesus fucking Christ, Edgar!"

Edgar held Simon's hips in a death grip. "You really want me to stop?"

"Fuck no!" His ass burned. He felt split in two, but that was what he wanted—to be taken as thoroughly as he could.

"Then shut up."

Simon shoved back against Edgar, making clear what he wanted, and Edgar obliged, thrusting over and over, hard enough to make Simon's head swim. He lowered his head to the mattress, no longer able to support himself on his arms. Simon reached between his legs to grab his own dick, but Edgar batted his hand away. "Not yet."

***

Sassy little shit. He wasn't going to take control back, not this time. He wanted to draw things out, make Simon lose his fucking mind, but Edgar didn't know how much longer he could last. Simon's ass was so fucking tight around his cock. A few times, he was jolted back to reality. *Oh my God. I'm fucking a guy in his ass.* But nothing about it felt unnatural. This was Simon and Simon was what he wanted.

Edgar reached under Simon now and worked his cock, but he slowed his fucking, torturing them both.

Simon whimpered. "Please. I'm so close, so fucking close. Where'd you learn to fuck like that?"

Edgar laughed and thrust hard, making Simon gasp.

"Yes. God, yes. Just like that." Simon tilted his hips, as if begging for Edgar to go deeper. "Don't make me wait. I'll do anything."

Simon tightened his ass around Edgar's dick, and heat seared down Edgar's spine. He couldn't hold back. He was going to... "Si!" Edgar drove in, barely managing to keep jacking Simon's cock as he shot his load.

Simon's started coming before Edgar was done.

"Too much," Simon muttered a few seconds later

as he pushed Edgar's hand away.

They both collapsed against the bed, wrung out. When Edgar thought he could move, he forced himself to pull out and sit up.

Simon gasped and his hand went to his side. "I think you may have killed me."

Edgar was hit with guilt. What the hell had he done? He'd gone at Simon like a rabid beast, forgetting completely about his wound at the end, only wanting to make sure his ass was sore enough that he wouldn't forget what Edgar could do to him.

"Are you okay? Let me see." Edgar pushed at Simon's hips, encouraging him to roll over.

"I'm fine. I didn't even feel anything until you sat up." But when Simon pulled his hand away from his side, there was blood on it.

"Oh fuck, I ripped your stitches."

Simon grinned as he rolled to his back.

"Shut up, you bastard." Edgar scowled as he inspected the wound. "Don't tell me you're happy about that."

"Don't tell me you're not proud of your manly skills?"

"Ha!" Edgar blew him off, but Simon was right. Edgar might be a right bastard for it, but the fact that he could make Simon so lost in the moment that he hadn't noticed the pain—yeah, he was proud of that.

"Will I live?"

Edgar nodded. "Yes. I should sew you back up, though."

Simon groaned and laid a hand over his eyes. "Haven't you tortured me enough?"

"Not even close."

***

When Edgar had finished patching Simon up, he lay back down on the bed and stretched out so close Simon could feel his heat. So what happened now? Between the pain in his side and the intensity of his reaction to Edgar, he was in desperate need of a distraction. "Was that weird. I mean, since you'd never... Since it was your first, uh..."

"God, Si, for a man who's made more conquests than he can count, you're having a hell of a time asking if it was weird for me to fuck a man or not."

Heat filled Simon's face.

Why is it so hard?

Because it's Edgar. Because it matters.

"Fine. Was your first time fucking a man strange?"

Edgar leaned his head to the side and quirked up his lip.

Simon hated feeling uncertain. He was used to being confident as hell in bed.

"A little. But not gross or anything."

That was it. Seriously? "I wouldn't think you'd come like that from gross sex." Fuck, he sounded so snippy.

Edgar grinned. "No, and his partner doesn't beg for more if he isn't doing things right either."

Simon realized Edgar was playing him. "You fucking loved it. And Jesus, you were good. My ass will be feeling that for a long time."

"Good." Edgar looked disturbingly smug.

"No apologies for the stitches?"

Edgar raised a brow. "Si. I've seen what you put yourself through on mission. A rough fuck and a

116

couple of popped stitches aren't going to do you any real damage."

Si couldn't decide if he was pleased that Edgar wasn't being overprotective or disappointed. "Damn right, it's not. Like I said, I like when it hurts, not too much, though. I'm not into whips or anything. Although there was this one guy—"

Edgar rolled Simon over and pinned him. "I do not want to hear about any other men."

Simon swallowed hard before trying to brush off what sounded like a declaration of exclusivity. Edgar couldn't really want that. "What about women?"

"No, Si. It's you and me now and that's all."

Simon's heart pounded. "Wait. You're serious?"

"I don't share." Edgar's expression was hard, challenging.

Simon huffed. "Of course you don't. But when I'm on a mission, I can't make any guarantees. I use any means necessary—"

"Yes, and one of your 'means' has been fucking, but not anymore," Edgar said with a growl.

Anger sizzled in Simon. Edgar taking control in bed was one thing, but no fucking way was he running Simon's life. "You can't tell me how to do my job."

"I don't want to tell you *how* to do your job. I want to tell you not to do it at all."

"Wait. You're asking me to quit?"

Edgar rolled over and laid his hand across his face "This is why I told you not to come back."

"Because you can't date me and me still be an operative?"

"Date? That's what you call this? Dating? You

said when you finally came to the bottom of all the lies surrounding the sinking of the *Ridgeway*, you'd be done."

"I lied." Simon was lying now. He had intended to lay down his weapons when this mission—the only mission he'd ever really considered his own—ended, but the idea of a regular life, of having what normal people dreamed of, terrified him.

Edgar rolled off the bed and headed for the bathroom. Simon heard the shower running and then several minutes later, Edgar came back with a towel wrapped around his waist and his hair dripping.

"Take a shower if you want," Edgar said. "Then you're going to tell me everything about what happened in DC, the fucking mission you were just on, and what you think we're going to find in Suffolk. I'm fucking tired of secrets."

Simon couldn't do that. His whole life was about secrets. "It's better to compartmentalize. We shouldn't all know—"

"Bullshit. You can fuck with me in bed but not anywhere else."

"Edgar, I'm not—"

"Get cleaned up."

Si hated feeling like a fucking coward, like he was coming apart. Part of him wanted to try to be someone better, someone Edgar could really love, but what if he fucked it all up?

CHAPTER ELEVEN

Edgar sat in the kitchen drinking a cup of coffee and waiting for Simon to get out of the shower. The bastard had been in there for ages. Either he was jerking off, which after just coming twice seemed unlikely, he'd taken up shaving his legs, or he was stalling. Door number three seemed the best choice. How could a man go into an enemy compound barely armed, with no backup, or single-handedly rescue three kidnapping victims with no support, but be terrified of having a relationship?

Aren't you just as afraid?

I was afraid of losing him. I still am, but I'm not afraid of trying.

Are you sure? Aren't all these rules of yours an attempt to push him away?

Sometimes Edgar really hated the thoughts that lurked in the recesses of his mind. He refused to continue that line of thinking. Fortunately he didn't have to because Simon had finally finished his shower.

He stalked into the kitchen, wearing new clothes instead of Edgar's now. "I won't quit, not even for you. I know you don't understand, but I…"

"Have to get revenge?"

"Justice, Edgar. It's fucking justice."

Edgar nodded. Si was right and he wanted that

justice too, but once Kingsford was dead—there would be no bringing him in to let the courts sort him out, Edgar was sure of that—he wasn't sure Si would really stop being an operative then.

"I want to kill the bastards who dared to take out my crew. Those men and women were my responsibility."

"You were so fucking young, Si, and you still saved most of your crew. That's what matters."

"But I couldn't save all of them."

Edgar stood and pulled Simon into his arms. How could he stay pissed off at him when Si was still hurting over what had happened? "They volunteered to stay. They knew the drill."

"I have to see this through. Can't you understand? Don't you want to make them pay?"

Edgar tightened his hold on Simon when he tried to push away. "I do. I want them as much as you do, but I'm worried about what this fight will do to you. Will you really ever be able to let it go? Once you have Kingsford, will you keep looking for anyone who worked with him, anyone connected, no matter how low they ranked?"

Simon broke Edgar's hold and stepped back. "I don't know. What the fuck else am I supposed to do?"

"You expect me to just be okay with you taking jobs no one else will, selling yourself to the highest bidder?"

Simon gave a bitter laugh. "It's not really like that."

What was that supposed to mean? If that wasn't what he'd been doing... "You told me—"

"You of all people should know I don't always tell the truth."

Edgar clenched his fists. "So you lied to me?" *Do not punch the son of a bitch.* "Again."

"I… stretched the truth."

Edgar slammed a hand down on the kitchen counter. "What the hell have you been doing? Not that I'll believe a word you say."

"Things you wouldn't approve of. But everything, every single fucking job I've taken, has been for this end. I agreed to any mission that could give me some intel on this organization, even if I thought the connection was remote. Danny and me, we've only really been on one mission for the last five years. To bring down this whole fucking organization if we have to do it one man at a time. Sometimes we take unrelated jobs, but those are all for funding this search, ending the shit Danny was assigned to over six years ago."

Edgar should have seen it, should have known Simon would never simply be a mercenary, not even after those CIA bastards had fucked with his head. He laid a hand on Simon's shoulder. "I'm sorry."

Simon ignored him. "Have you ever noticed I don't live like a fucking top-dollar assassin? I put everything back into my real mission. It's not like the CIA is bankrolling even half the shit we're doing."

"Simon, please."

Si held up his hand and kept going. "My soul is black as hell and I'll probably never be able to live a normal life, but if I can end this, then it will all be worth it, even if you hate me for what I have to do."

"Si, these men deserve to die, painfully. Nothing

you do to end them could possibly make me hate you."

"But some of what I've done to get this far. If you knew…" He turned away.

Edgar wanted to comfort him, to swear that he would love Simon no matter what, but a dark part of his mind wondered if this were more manipulation. "How am I supposed to know what's real with you?"

Simon shook his head. "I don't know."

"Do you still remember how to tell the truth?"

Simon shrugged.

Edgar wondered if he should hand over the mission supplies and send Simon on his way, but right or wrong, he'd never do that. He loved Simon and he'd known exactly what Simon was from day one, a man determined to save others no matter the consequences to himself.

He took Simon by the arm and led him to the couch. When they were seated, he laid a hand on his thigh and said, "Talk to me."

Simon shifted position, lying down and putting his head in Edgar's lap. They'd lain like this many times as friends, but now it felt far more intimate. Edgar ran his fingers through Simon's hair. They were so screwed. Neither of them had any idea how to proceed with a relationship. Was there any hope for them?

Simon sighed. "Sometimes I think you should've let me die."

No. No way in hell was he going there. "No, Simon, I—"

Simon waved him off. "But then I think maybe the reason I lived was so I could do this. Pull all these threads together and end this once and for all."

"Simon, I saved you because I loved you. You were my best friend and now you're even more. Your worth doesn't end when these men are dead. If you start believing that, then they've won."

"What are the chances we'll all make it out of this alive?"

Simon looked so sad, so defeated. Edgar wanted to shake him until he saw reason, until the brightness came back into his eyes. "We may not survive, but that doesn't mean any of us have to deliberately sacrifice ourselves."

"That's not what I'm planning to do."

Edgar caressed the side of his face. "Are you sure?"

Simon closed his eyes. "Only if I have to."

Simon shivered, and Edgar grabbed a blanket and laid it over him. "You're afraid, more so than I've ever seen you."

"What if Kingsford or some of his associates get away? What if we can't uncover all the layers? What if this goes on forever? I... I don't know how much longer I can last."

"Some of the pieces may never be found. You might have to accept that."

"But I can't stop until it's done."

Edgar pulled Simon onto his lap and encouraged him to lay his head on Edgar's shoulder. "Simon, you can't do that to yourself."

"I'm not. That order came from the C I fucking A."

Edgar wished he'd killed the fuckers who "rescued" him and Si when he had the chance.

"Simon, they mind-fucked you, and I don't think you've ever accepted how badly."

"I… Those days, in that place, without you. The things they said. I was in so much pain, and I… I can't remember it all."

As much as Edgar thought he was probably better off not knowing exactly what those assholes had done to Simon, he wasn't sure that was what Simon needed. He wished Laura were there to help him say the right thing.

"When I woke up and they were there, I didn't know if they were enemies or friends or where the fuck they came from. I… I begged for you and they told me you'd left—"

"I would never leave you." Edgar realized how true those words were.

"I knew that and I fought. I was bleeding all over the place, so much blood, just like on the ship, but you weren't there."

If Edgar ever found these men, he would rip them apart with his bare hands and stomp on the pieces.

***

Simon grabbed at Edgar's hand, trying to anchor himself, but the memories were too strong. They pulled him under until he was there again, imprisoned and alone.

"We could have caught those terrorists if you'd cooperated."

These bastards who were interrogating him had strapped his arms to the bed and he was too weak to get free. "Cooperated? You mean died. Let all my men die. Fuck you. You son of—"

"By stopping them from reaching their objective, you tipped them off." The man's voice was eerily calm, and Simon wanted to rip his tongue out.

"How long had you been planning to sacrifice my ship? Is that why they gave me a fucking ship to start with?"

All the asshole did was smile.

Simon kicked him in the gut. He stumbled back and Simon struggled to get free, but the other man in the room, the one who looked like a boy but was even more ruthless than his partner, subdued him. He called for more restraints and Simon's ankles were cuffed.

Simon's head spun as he dropped back against the pillow. He looked down. Blood was soaking through his hospital gown. But that didn't matter. Edgar would heal him when he got free. He would get free. He had to. These men couldn't be CIA, they…

The world started to go black.

The man he'd kicked leaned over him. "You'll regret this," he promised.

Simon passed out then.

"Si?" He thought he heard Edgar's voice, but he couldn't zero in on it.

"No. Just a dream. Not here." Edgar couldn't be there. They'd taken Edgar from him.

Later, when he was awake again, untied this time—possibly they thought he was too weak to fight anymore—the darker man returned. He ignored everything Simon said, but at least he didn't give Simon the creeps the way the boyish one did. "Simon McLeod is dead," he'd explained. "You'll have a new identity now and you'll work for us."

"I'm not dead. I'm sitting right here." He was alive. He could feel his heart beating. Unless it was all a trick and he was in hell.

The man shook his head. "As far as the rest of the world is concerned, you don't exist anymore."

"I'm Simon McLeod. I'm a captain in the US Navy."

The man shook his head. "Not anymore, you're not."

He'd lost it then, punching the man in the face. The man had grabbed his arm and bent it back until Simon heard something in his wrist snap. Pain shot up his arm. He clutched the bed and retched over the side while the man laughed.

"Si! Si! I'm right here."

"Edgar?"

"Yes, baby. Come back to me." He held Simon tight while he sobbed. "He broke my fucking arm."

"Oh, Si." Edgar stroked the arm in question. Simon had never told him how it had happened. He only knew it had been a bad break and it still ached when Simon overused it.

"They don't have any hold over you now," Edgar said, trying to soothe him.

"But they do. They always will until I end this."

"Were those men really CIA?"

"Yes, but... I'm not sure if what they did was sanctioned or some black op where they went off the rails."

"What about Derrick? Who does he really work for?"

"I'm not sure. That's one of the things that's killing me. Derrick is the one who helped me break away from them. I'll always owe him for that, but Danny thinks Derrick's been compromised, that he's being blackmailed. He has a family. If they got to them…"

Edgar sighed. "Is this weekend a suicide mission?"

Simon shrugged. "If it turns out that way, you're sure as hell not participating."

"And you are?"

"Kingsford isn't going to stop. He's going to keep taking money to let criminals and terrorists further their agenda without caring how many military, FBI, police, or civilians get in the way."

"And you still don't know their endgame?"

Simon didn't want to drop that bomb on Edgar, but he'd hear it soon enough. "Based on what I saw a few days ago, I think Kingsford's planning a military coup. Whether that's how this started or not, that's what it looks like now."

The color drained from Edgar's face. "Fuck me."

"Yeah. That about sums it up. See why we can't let this sit?"

CHAPTER TWELVE

Arguing with Simon about the mission would be like arguing with a rock. Edgar saw that. He just hoped that someday Simon would realize that he was more than a weapon. At least he could comfort Simon in other ways.

He lifted Simon off his lap and then knelt in front of him.

Simon's eyes widened. "Edgar?"

"For once just close your mouth and let me take care of you."

Edgar tugged at the sweatpants Simon was wearing. He pulled them down just enough to reveal Simon's cock. As soon as Edgar took it in his hand, it started to swell.

Simon wrapped a hand around Edgar's wrist but Edgar wasn't sure if Simon was trying to stop him or make him stroke Simon's cock faster. "Edgar, you don't have to do this."

"I want to. I've wondered what sucking your cock would be like ever since I admitted to myself that I wanted you. All of you. I'm going to find out right now, and unless it's to make those goddamn sexy noises you made earlier, don't open your mouth."

"Fuck" was the only reply Simon made.

Simon was fully hard now, and Edgar hoped to

God he could do this right, make it good for Simon. He was more than a little afraid he might not be able to follow through with his promise, but he was sure as hell going to make a good effort.

He leaned down and ran his tongue along Simon's length. The soft skin and hardness underneath felt interesting to his tongue, not at all bad. He dipped his tongue into Simon's slit.

"Edgar!" Simon gasped.

He did it again. *Okay, here goes.* He took Simon's shaft into his mouth, sucking him the way he himself liked to be sucked. Apparently, Simon liked it too. Edgar looked up at Si. His eyes were closed and he'd sunk his teeth into his lower lip. So far so good. Edgar kept going, realizing he liked the feel of Simon in his mouth, liked what it did to Simon. He used his hand to work the base of Simon's shaft, stroking as he sucked. Simon shifted under him, like he was fighting not to thrust.

Simon opened his eyes when Edgar took him deeper. Edgar smiled around the shaft in his mouth. Simon jerked his hips and gasped. Perfect. The fear was gone from his eyes, replaced by lust.

He kept going, sucking and sliding his lips along Simon's cock. He forgot all about being worried. Simon's hands slid into Edgar's hair but he held still, letting Edgar take control. Edgar swallowed around him, fighting his gag reflex as he let Simon's cock slide deeper.

"Edgar. Oh my fucking God, you…"

This was exactly what he'd wanted, for Simon to let go and lose himself in pleasure.

Simon shifted his hips restlessly, and Edgar

pinned them down while using his mouth to tease Simon's cock and then his balls, lapping at them and nipping at the loose skin of his scrotum.

"Yes! God, yes! Edgar, please!"

Edgar teased Simon's perineum with his fingers and then pushed against Simon's entrance, finally entering him an inch or so. God, he was so fucking tight.

"More. Please, more!" Simon begged. Edgar finger-fucked him as he returned to sucking his cock.

Simon thrust hard enough to break Edgar's hold and Edgar backed off so he wasn't risking being choked, but he didn't stop. He wanted to drive Simon insane.

"Edgar. Fuck. Edgar, I'm going to…"

Edgar let Simon's cock slip from his mouth. He wasn't sure he was ready for swallowing even though part of him wanted to try. He added a second finger to Simon's ass and jacked him off, holding Simon's gaze as he worked him. Seconds later, Simon cried out and spunk shot from his cock.

Simon didn't look away even when Edgar saw fear flash into his eyes.

"Do you have any idea how hot you are with your lips swollen from sucking my dick?" Simon asked.

Edgar laughed. "I probably look like a fucking mess."

"You do and it's so hot." Simon sat up enough be able to pull his shirt off even though he winced as he did so. "I want to watch you jack off, and then I want you to come on me."

"What the fuck, Si?"

"Please, Edgar. I... I need that."

Simon was obviously not ready to face reality. Edgar didn't think Simon had ever begged for anything when someone didn't have a hand around his cock. Demanded. Expected. Sure. But he'd never asked Edgar for anything with that soft, pleading tone. No way in hell would Edgar deny him.

He stood and shucked his pants. Then he straddled Simon as Si scooted down so he was slumped on the couch. Simon smiled at him with that grin that melted him. Every. Fucking. Time.

"You want to see me stroke my cock?" Edgar asked. "Watch me make myself come? You want to be covered in it?"

"God yes." Simon sighed the words like it was his idea of heaven.

Fuck. If only Edgar had known how good this would be. They could've been having sex for months, maybe years if he hadn't been such an idiot and hidden the truth from himself.

"Is this all real? You're not playing me now, are you?"

"What?" Simon's eyes widened in shock, but Edgar has seen him fake emotion so easily he'd forgotten Si was playing a role.

"Is. This. Real?"

"Fuck yes." Simon actually looked hurt. "I've lied to you, yeah, but not like this. I will never lie to you about us. I've never felt like this with any man or woman. I don't think I ever could again."

Edgar stopped talking then and focused on pleasure, jacking himself off faster and faster, need for Simon burning him up, making him feel like there was too much inside him, too much emotion to contain and…

"Holy fucking fuck!" His orgasm hit like a punch, taking his breath, making him gasp. He slipped and nearly landed on Simon. He caught himself on the back of the couch as he shot again and again, covering Simon's torso.

"Wow! That was so fucking hot." Simon ran his hand through one of the sticky white trails and then licked his fingers.

Edgar shuddered as he watched. "Si?"

Simon laid a finger on his lip. A finger still sticky with Edgar's own cum. "I don't want to argue."

"Me either. But I also don't want you to walk away."

"I won't, okay? But I've got to have my head in the game this weekend."

"Are you saying we're going to pretend like nothing has changed between us while we're at the lake?"

Simon frowned. "Can we please not talk about this now?"

Edgar nodded. "Fine, I'll give you a short reprieve."

Simon looked down at his abdomen and traced his finger in the mess. "You've really never wanted another man?"

Edgar shook his head. "I've noticed men who were hot and appreciated their bodies, but I've never seriously considered fucking a man other than you."

Simon smiled. "Good."

Edgar rolled his eyes. "Possessive asshole."

Simon sat up, pushing Edgar off him. "You're

one to talk."

Edgar stood and ran a hand through his hair. "We both need a shower before we pack up."

"Yeah." Simon brushed his hand over the sofa cushions. "You bitched at me about bleeding on your couch and now you've come on it."

"Fucking fuck."

Simon slapped Edgar's ass and laughed as he headed for the bathroom.

***

An hour later they were on the road to Edgar's lake house. Simon was in the passenger seat, and he hadn't been able to sit still for five seconds. He hated not driving, but Edgar refused to have him put any more strain on his side unless he had to defend himself. He'd pointed out that Edgar hadn't minded the strain fucking him had caused, but Edgar had just flipped him off and refused to reveal the location of his keys.

"If you're trying to make me regret driving, it's not working," Edgar said with a sickeningly sweet smile.

"It will by the time we're there." Simon was damn good at pissing people off.

"The drive only takes an hour and a half. I've put up with worse from you for much longer."

He had a point. "Fine, but could you at least get me a soda?"

"So you'll be even more revved up?"

"I've only had a few cups of coffee today."

"Si, we're not stopping. There are sodas in the back." Simon tried to reach one, but gasped and fell back against the seat, holding his side.

"Fuck it, Si." Edgar reached into the back seat and fiddled around until he found the right bag. He lifted it over the seat and handed it to Simon. "You're worse than a five-year-old in the car."

"Nope." Simon shook his head. "I remember road trips as a kid. This is not worse."

"I'm not talking about *you* as a kid. I mean a normal five-year-old."

"Huh." Simon cracked the seal on his drink bottle and it fizzed up, running over and wetting his leg.

"Don't fuck up my car," Edgar said.

"Quit your bitching."

The next few moments passed in silence except for Simon tapping his fingers on the console, which he knew irritated the shit out of Edgar. Eventually, Edgar asked, "How are we playing things when we get to the cabin?"

"What things?" Simon knew. He just wanted to make Edgar say it.

"The fact that we're fucking."

"Danny likely knows already."

"You told him?"

"No but he's been telling me to make a move on you since South America. He's likely guessed that something happened or you would've kicked me out."

"Since South America? What the fuck?"

"Danny saw more than either of us did, apparently."

"There wasn't an us when we were there."

Simon arched a brow when Edgar glanced at him.

"Okay, fine. There's always been an us but not with a sexual connection."

"Do you know how close I came to making a move on you after we got out of that fucking prison hole?"

Edgar glanced at Simon quickly again before focusing back on the road. Simon could feel the tension in the air pressing on his skin.

"I've wanted you since you walked on board my ship," he confessed.

"Fuck! I guess Danny saw everything, then."

"He'd be dead by now if he wasn't that observant."

"So we say nothing and let them figure it out." Edgar's hands tightened on the wheel.

"You're mine. They all know that. The fact that we're fucking now is irrelevant."

Edgar sputtered. "Jackson and Sport know?"

"Remember how I babysat Jackson's boyfriend, Addy?"

"Yeah."

"Well, by the end of the mission, I wasn't sure who was keeping who. He managed to get stories out of me that I've never told anyone but Danny. He put things together and decided I was in love with you."

"What the fuck did you tell him?"

"Not much, but he's smart. Good with puzzles."

Edgar sighed. "Is he in on this?"

"No, Jackson wouldn't risk him like that. He's damn good with tactics, but he doesn't belong in the field. He hardly knows one end of a gun from another."

"Who'll look after him this time? If we hurt these bastards, they'll go after all of us."

Simon nodded. "I know. I haven't asked, but I'm

sure Jackson has him somewhere safe. We've all been expecting these bastards to go on the offensive since DC, but nothing has happened so far." A shiver ran over Simon as he said those words. It wouldn't be long now. One way or another, things would come to a head.

CHAPTER THIRTEEN

Edgar and Simon had been at the cabin long enough for Edgar to move the supplies inside and unload groceries while Simon did a sweep of the perimeter.

"Something feels off," Si said when he stepped in the door.

"Off how?" Edgar had learned to trust Simon's instincts. He wouldn't go so far as to say Simon had some kind of psychic juju, but he often seemed to know things for which there was no concrete evidence.

"I can't see anyone out there now, but I saw a lot of broken twigs and flattened ground cover as if someone had walked through recently."

"Animals? There are bears around here."

Simon shook his head. "I'm not a tracker, not an expert one at least, but I don't think so. Someone has been watching the house. They know we're gathering here."

"Is that what your gut tells you?"

Simon nodded. "We need to have someone on watch while we're here. I'm sorry. I thought someone would try to tail us and I was on guard for that, but apparently they were already watching the place."

"There was only so much we could do to hide who the real owner of this cabin is. And once they traced it to me—"

"They knew it was the perfect place for us to meet."

Edgar nodded. "But how did they know a strike would be our next move? Wouldn't the men who captured you assume we'd go after them, rather than poke into Kingsford's retreat?"

"They're obviously fucking good, considering what they've gotten away with and how long it's taken us to get close," Simon responded.

"Still, we moved fast. What if...?" Edgar hated to even think it.

"There's someone on the inside?" Si asked.

"Yeah." Suddenly, Edgar didn't want any of the coffee he'd started. The idea of a betrayal by someone they considered a friend made him queasy. "Derrick?" he asked.

Simon frowned. "I never checked in with him, so he doesn't know what I learned."

"But he'd know that you escaped if he's working with them. If not him, then who?"

Simon shook his head.

Edgar stomach flip-flopped as he considered whether they could completely trust the men who would be arriving soon. "What if it's someone even closer?"

Simon looked up from his mug, horror on his face. "Not Danny. No, you can't—"

Edgar held up a hand. "No, but Jackson—"

Si shook his head. "You haven't met him. He's on our side and so is Sport. Danny would know if he wasn't. I'd stake my life on their loyalty."

"Which we're about to do."

"Their teammate was killed. Jackson came close to losing his leg."

Edgar held up a hand. "I know the story, and I hate having to suspect everyone, but—"

"It's not them. If it's anyone… Maybe Kingsford's men are just that good. Maybe I'm losing it."

"No, you're as good as ever. But it's possible we're up against people as good as you are with better resources. We have to face that."

Si exhaled loudly. "I don't like either of those options." He stood and placed his mug in the sink. "I'll go stand guard."

Edgar watched Simon walk away. He wanted to drag him back, wrap his arms around him, and kiss him until they both forgot how bad their odds were.

***

Danny and the man Edgar assumed was Special Agent Cranford, aka Sport, arrived a few minutes later. The cabin seemed to shrink when they entered. Sport was a big man, and the force of Danny's personality was enough to fill any room. While Danny didn't inspire the intensity of lust that Simon did, Edgar appreciated just how hot he was. Danny was at least as good at seduction as Simon if not better. And he was darkness to Simon's sunny good looks, the bad boy you couldn't resist rather than the all-American sailor.

Sport was as attractive as Danny, but he looked less like he might eat you. He held out his hand to Edgar. "Hugh Cranford. Nice to meet you."

"I'm Edgar. Simon's been telling me a lot about you."

Sport laughed. "Don't listen to any of it."

"I've learned to take anything Simon says with a grain of salt or maybe a whole jar."

Si flipped him off. "Where's Jackson?"

"He's on his way. He had to drop Addy off with a friend."

"A friend?" Simon asked. "Is that a good idea?"

"A friend of mine," Danny said. Simon narrowed his eyes at him, obviously wanting more details, but Danny turned to Edgar instead. "Is he okay? Really?" He tilted his head toward Simon.

Simon scowled at them both. "I can speak for myself."

"And tell the truth?" Danny had him there.

"He's patched up. Should he be here? No. Can he hold his own in a fight? Yeah, as long as things don't get too intense. He needs time, but—"

"We don't have it," Danny finished.

"Have you learned anything new?" Simon asked.

Danny shook his head. "Not really. Reed has eyes on the place. No movement, but ideally, we'll be in and out tonight. They could come back any time."

"How sure are we that this is the right place?" Edgar asked. He wasn't usually one to talk about gut instincts, but something felt wrong about this whole mission. Maybe it was nothing but nerves.

Simon chewed his lip for a few seconds before answering. "I wish I could say I'm certain, but all I've got to go on is the men who captured me talking about The Retreat and how operations were going well there and something about moving to a new facility."

"If Kingsford's there, he'll know we're on to

him," Edgar pointed out.

"If he's hiding out, he hasn't got many reinforcements. No signs of life in the house and no one in and out for days," Danny said.

Edgar still wasn't convinced. "Even if that was the case, he has to have men watching the place or some defenses set up."

"True, but after what I heard, I've got to check it out."

Edgar nodded. "I know. And you don't have to do it alone." He didn't want Simon to ever feel alone again.

Simon nodded. "I can't let anything go at this point. I feel like time is running out. Kingsford has to be caught before he pulls something else."

"Trust me, this matters to us as much as it does to you," Sport said.

Si looked at Sport, studying him hard. "I wouldn't have thought that was possible, but maybe you really do understand how much this matters."

Sport nodded. "We've both lost a hell of lot—friends, careers, maybe our fucking sanity."

Simon was about to say something when the sound of gravel crunching made him pause. "A car."

Everyone drew their weapons. At Simon's direction, he and Sport moved toward the door while Danny and Edgar took up positions on either side of the window.

"It's Jackson," Sport announced, sounding relieved.

Edgar watched as a tall, lean man got out of the car. "You assholes better not shoot me," the man, obviously Jackson, yelled. "I had to argue with some son of a bitch at the rental car office, and I'm in no mood to have to kill all of you."

"Yeah, that certainly is Jackson." Danny laughed. "I've fucking missed him."

Edgar could tell the next few hours were going to be interesting. "Si says Jackson's mouth is even trashier than yours."

Danny glared at Simon. "I'm offended. But… he might be right."

All the men laughed.

When Jackson stepped through the door, he and Sport embraced. Then he acknowledged the others. "Danny, Simon, good to see you." His gaze fell on Edgar and Edgar could see him doing an assessment, just like Simon had warned.

"Are you done staring? I feel like I should get dinner first if you're going to eye-fuck me any longer."

Jackson grinned. "Nah, you'll do. I'd have to put Simon down if I tried anything serious with you, and like I said, I'm not in the mood."

Sport raised a brow. "Should I call Addy now?"

"Fuck no." Jackson shook his head. "He's not Addy's type."

"Oh really?" Edgar asked.

Simon stepped in front of Edgar then. "He's mine."

Jackson studied the two of them for a few seconds. "Great. So I get to listen to you two fucking as well as those assholes." He gestured toward Sport and Danny. "This is gonna be one hell of a weekend."

"You're welcome to watch," Danny said.

Sport made an exclamation of disgust. "No.

You're not."

"He'll be too busy Skype-sexing Addy anyway," Simon insisted.

Edgar cleared his throat. "Now that we've all marked our territory. We need to update you on what Si found when we got here."

Sport frowned. "What's up?"

"Someone's been watching this place."

"Fucking bastards, are you sure?" Danny asked.

"When I walked the perimeter, I found branches broken, leaves flattened, and cigarette butts scattered."

"Could have just been some kids from another lake house drinking or fucking in the woods," Sport pointed out.

"Yeah, but it feels off. No trash, no beer bottles, no condom wrappers. Kids leave shit behind."

"Do we need to change location?" Sport asked.

"Maybe or we might just need to be careful."

"We need to get this the fuck over with," Jackson said.

"So let's make a plan," Sport suggested. "We can't go in there blind. I know fuck-all right now except that Kingsford's supposed to have been doing some kind of research—into what, I don't know—in this vacation house of his. We've got the layout of the house, but we need to decide how to approach and what exactly we're looking for if we're going to get in and out quickly. There are too many places to get trapped around there. Water on one side and woods on the other."

"I doubt they'd shoot at us across a public lake," Danny said. "They seem to be trying to keep a low profile."

"That could depend on what we find and how much they want to cover it up," Edgar said.

"If Kingsford's been running this shit from the beginning, we know he's damn good at making anyone who gets in his way look like they're the ones to blame for the incident."

Si nodded. "If he arranged to have my ship sunk, then the men that planned to let me die might've been working with him. They may have intended to lay any number of crimes on me. The fucking goons who claimed to be rescuing me threatened to make it look like I was to blame for the whole incident, like I was a fucking traitor."

"What?" Anger rushed through Edgar. Every time Si revealed more about what happened after Edgar had been sedated and put on a plane for the States, he hated the men who'd "rescued" them more.

"They told me I had to cooperate and let them declare me dead or I'd be court-martialed."

"So they punished you for failing to die," Danny said. "Typical."

Edgar didn't know how they could discuss this shit so calmly. "Those sons of bitches! How dare they—"

Simon touched his arm. "Don't. They don't deserve your energy. We need to focus on the present. We'll get Kingsford, and his minions will fall with him."

"Goddamn right they will."

Simon smiled at him. "I knew you wanted in on this."

"What I want is all of us out of this game, and the

only way to do that is to follow this trail to the end."

Simon skimmed his fingers down the underside of Edgar's arm. "We'll get out. I want more time with you."

Jackson pretended to gag. "You two can go fuck after we make a plan, but please try to refrain from doing it in front of me."

Simon flipped him off, but Danny purred. "I wouldn't mind watching."

"You're such a fucking slut," Jackson said.

Sport massaged Danny's shoulders, pulling his man back against him. "That does occasionally have its advantages."

"Fucking fuck shit!" Jackson grumbled. "Am I really going to have to put up with this the whole time I'm here? Congratulations, by the way," he said, looking at Simon.

"For what?"

"Finding the balls to stop pining for Edgar and do something about it."

"Actually, I was the one who did something," Edgar said. "Simon was still being a pussy."

Danny laughed. "That doesn't surprise me."

Simon stomped into the kitchen and started rummaging in the snack cabinet. "I hate you all. Every single fucking one of you."

"Can we get down to business?" Sport asked. "We are on the clock here."

"Yes, sir. Mr. Special Agent, sir," Danny quipped. "I actually do have a plan. Kind of."

"Yeah, I've heard it. It's fucking weak," Sport said. "Simon, what have you got?"

Simon shook his head. "Not much. I like to

improvise."

"I like to not die," Jackson said.

"You SEALs," Danny tsked. "Always going by the book."

Jackson took a step toward him. "The fuck we do." If tensions were already running this high, Edgar wondered how the hell they'd make it through the next day.

Sport laid a hand on Jackson's shoulder. "I think 'the book' went out a long time ago on this one, but that doesn't mean I intend to go in blind. You captained a fucking ship, Simon. You're telling me you can't make an attack plan?"

"I've been on my own for long fucking time, and things never go the way they're planned," Simon answered.

Sport shook his head. "That's why you make contingencies."

Edgar had had enough. "Can we please stop standing around arguing and get on with it? We're never going to decide anything sniping at each other."

"Fine," Simon huffed.

Sport rolled a paper out on the table. "Here's the map of the house. Reed was able to get real-time satellite images. There aren't any cars there and there haven't been any for the last day."

"Luck or a setup?" Jackson asked.

Danny shrugged. "Could go either way. That's the fun of it."

Sport shoved at Danny's shoulder. "There's nothing fun about this shit, you asshole."

"Oh right, you're one of those who claims not to love the thrill of the chase."

Edgar's respect for Sport doubled after that comment. "At least one of you has some fucking sense. I want these men to pay. I want to save everyone I can from the hell we've experienced, but I don't need to risk my life every day to be fulfilled."

"No," Simon said, a dirty grin on his face. "That's not what gets Edgar hard."

"Don't push me," Jackson warned.

"I say we go in from here." Danny pointed to a spot on the map.

Jackson shook his head. "We'd have a tactical advantage if we used the trees here for cover." He pointed to a spot farther west.

"So we're going for covert rather than outright storming the place?" Danny asked.

Jackson rolled his eyes. "Fuck yes. The idea is that no one knows we're there."

"The idea is to get the hell in and out as fast as we can," Danny said.

Edgar was ready to rip his hair out. "There are too many fuckers in this room who think they're in charge. We've got to be a team for this, not a bunch of alphas measuring their dicks."

"I'm taking point on this," Simon said. "Fucking Kingsford is mine."

Edgar laid a hand on Simon's shoulder. "From what we can see, it's very unlikely Kingsford himself is there even if someone else is. If he is there and it's a setup, we're not likely to come out on top. If he's not there, then at best we'll get some intel."

"Potentially a fuckload of intel if the men who captured me had it right."

Jackson scoffed. "You really think they've left it

there for us to find. If only we could be that lucky."

Danny grinned. "I got the luck of the Irish, love."

"You've got the luck of your silver tongue and your hard dick. That's about it."

"Fuck off."

Edgar stepped back and ran his hands through his hair. "Can I just shoot myself now and save Kingsford's men the trouble?"

Simon took his hand and squeezed it. "We'll go with Jackson's plan and use the tree cover. How's that?"

Before they could answer, Sport moved toward the window. "Someone's there. Eleven o'clock. In the woods. I'm going out the back to circle around."

Sport was out the door, weapon drawn before anyone could ask more questions. Jackson headed out right behind him, but Simon stopped him with a hand on his shoulder. "You're better at long range than me. I'll go with Sport. You stay and be ready if we need you."

Jackson looked like he wanted to argue. Edgar could tell he was not used to taking orders. "Fine."

Edgar didn't want to think about how Simon was heading into a complete unknown situation. "They won't just shoot this guy and ask questions later, will they?"

Danny shrugged.

"For fuck's sake. It could be one of my neighbors."

"Do the neighbors like to wear camo and arm themselves to the fucking teeth?"

Danny had a point. "Not usually."

Jackson passed Edgar a pair of binoculars. When

he looked through them toward the woods, he could just make out a human form. The man, assuming the form was male, blended with the woods. Edgar could only see him because he knew he was there. He could, however, see the glint off a rifle's barrel and what looked like the outline of a shoulder holster. "How the fuck did Sport even spot this guy?"

"He's that good."

"He's the fucking best."

Jackson's and Danny's words ran into each other.

Edgar looked from one of them to the other. "Are you sure you three aren't all fucking each other?"

"I appreciate what he's got," Jackson said, brazenly checking Danny out. "But no. Dealing with Danny's not an easy job or at least it doesn't sound like it when Sport's making him cry like a little girl."

"Fuck you!" Danny said, but he was laughing.

Edgar had never quite gotten the knack of joking around like that when his people were walking into danger, but for most operatives it seemed to ease the tension.

CHAPTER FOURTEEN

Simon followed Sport deep into the woods, neither of them making a sound. Simon knew without having to ask that they were planning to come up behind the man. Simon wanted to be wrong about them being watched. He wanted the man Sport had caught sight of to simply be a visitor to the lake out for a walk, but they didn't have that kind of luck.

Within a few seconds after turning back toward the lakeshore, they spotted the man. He was wearing camo. He had two pistols in a shoulder holster and was sighting through a rifle. Simon drew his weapon and flicked off the safety.

The man turned then. The slightest movement of his arm told Si he was about to shoot. Before he got off a shot, Sport hit him dead center in the chest. He stumbled and went down to his knees but he turned, aiming toward them again. Si shot him in the leg. If they could make him talk, he'd be a valuable prisoner.

As they ran toward him, the man raised up and reached for one of his pistols, but Si landed a kick to his jaw. He flew back and Sport trained his gun on the man. "Don't even think about moving. I can put a bullet through your brain before your hand touches a weapon." Simon circled him, trying to assess his physical condition. Sport's shot had hit his thigh and his pants were soaked with blood but not enough to kill him. He must have been wearing a vest because Simon didn't see anything but a rip in the fabric of his jacket. No blood and if he'd been hit there, he'd be feeling it. Sport kicked the rifle toward Si and then took the pistols from the man's holster.

"Stand up," he ordered. The man looked at Sport, and Sport nodded.

Simon checked him for other weapons, extracting another small pistol and two knives. This was a man who liked to be prepared.

"Who the fuck are you?" Sport asked.

The man just laughed. "If you don't know, I'm sure as fuck not going to tell you, am I?"

Sport gestured with his gun. "I'd be happy to shoot you again."

"Nah, FBI, you won't take the shot, not when I'm already under your power."

Fuck! The asshole knew who they were. They needed to get him back to the cabin for questioning and that wasn't going to be easy without any cuffs. The man was right, Sport wouldn't shoot him, but Si had no trouble putting him out of commission. He slammed the butt of his pistol down on the back of the man's head and he slumped forward, his weight nearly pulling Simon over on top of him. Damn, he was a big, thick son of a bitch.

"How likely do you think it is some neighbor heard that and called the police?" Si asked.

"High enough that we need to get out of here as fucking fast as we can." Sport lifted the man over his shoulder. "I'm counting on you to have my back if he has buddies out here."

Si nodded, taking the rear as Sport worked his way back through the woods, clearly not wanting to risk the open lawn that would have made a more direct route.

"Everything okay in here?" Simon asked as they stepped into the cabin.

"We're good," Jackson answered as he helped Sport lower the man to the floor. "Who is this fucker?"

"We don't know, but he knew who *I* was."

"Fuck!" Danny said. "We should get out of here. Right fucking now."

"*Or* we could stay until he's conscious and we can question him," Simon responded. "We know to watch out now. Maybe we can get something out of this asshole and not have to scrap this mission."

Danny frowned, looking uncharacteristically rattled. "No, we get someone to pick him up and take him in for interrogation. We're not safe here. Trying to secure this location now would be a nightmare. We should move to a hotel or some other neutral ground."

"Where they may be just as likely to find us. At least we know to be on guard here," Simon pointed out.

"The devil you know?" Jackson asked.

"I don't like knowing any devils who are fucking shooting at us," Edgar said. "But stay or go, this man needs medical attention."

"He needs to be cuffed and then we need to wake him up and make him start talking," Simon said.

"Si, I'm going to help this man. He's got a bullet in him." Edgar bent to examine the man's leg.

"One might've been in you if we hadn't brought

Silvia Violet

the fucker down."

Anger sizzled in Edgar's eyes when he looked at Simon. "If you think I'm not grateful for that, you're wrong, but we don't let prisoners suffer. That's not who we are."

"Make sure he's not going to bleed out while we pack the gear," Danny said. "Then we're getting the fuck out of here."

"Where are we going to go?" Sport asked. "There's nothing around here."

"We could break into The Retreat now," Jackson suggested. "If at least some of Kingsford's men are busy looking for us here, we can attack while they think we're trying to find another hidey-hole."

"If they're watching us, then this mission is fucked," Edgar said. "They're not just going to let us walk away with this intel."

Danny shrugged. "So we'll hide for a while."

"Some of us have jobs to return to," Sport reminded them.

Danny waved a hand dismissively. "You're on extended leave."

"Says who?" Sport asked.

"Your boss."

Sport studied Danny.

"He's on his way to meet us. We need him."

Si couldn't believe it. Darrow, Sport's Special Agent in Charge, was supposed to do everything he could to stay off the radar. "Fuck, Danny. If he joins us in the field, the chances of him being linked to this shit go way up."

"He thinks it's worth the risk this time."

Simon shook his head. "Goddammit. Edgar,

how's this fucker doing?"

Edgar looked up from his patient. "Not good."

"Will he live? Because if so, we need to go," Danny said.

"Fuck, Danny! Have some respect," Sport said. "Edgar actually gives a damn about helping people. He's a fucking doctor, not an assassin."

Hurt showed on Danny's face for a moment and Simon braced himself for a nasty fight, but Danny turned and stared out the window. "We don't know how many more of these bastards are out there."

Edgar looked at Simon, and Si hated how exhausted and sad he looked. "If we leave him with water, he'll survive. I'll give him a sedative."

Simon laid a hand on his shoulder. "You're doing more than most people would."

Edgar glared at him. "I fucking hate this."

He'd always had such a big heart. He'd killed when he needed to, but every single time they'd hurt people, a piece of him had died. He didn't belong in this world. "I know you do."

Edgar shook his head. "You just had to come to me, didn't you? You had to show up on my doorstep looking so fucking cute."

Edgar had every right to be angry, but Simon was too edgy to let him rant and ignore it. "You agreed to help. You want these men to pay, I know you do, and you knew—"

"That things always go to shit when you're around? Yeah, I did. There's a reason I quit this life."

"And a reason you got back in," Sport said, laying a hand on Edgar's shoulder.

Edgar turned and looked at him. He looked

sincere, calm, caring. He must be a fucking terrific federal agent. People would talk to him and he would help them feel safe. "Yeah, there is."

"You're doing the right thing, but we need to go now. The gear's almost packed."

Simon brought in several of the water bottles and laid them by the man who was currently on the kitchen floor.

"You realize if the police investigate and find him here, we're going to be top suspects," Sport pointed out.

"I've already got someone on the way to clean up after us," Danny said.

Sport frowned. "Sometimes, you still scare me."

Fuck! Danny was just as screwed up as he was. What chance did he have for a relationship if Danny and Sport could barely keep it together?

Edgar stuffed some pillows under the man's legs to elevate them, and Simon cuffed his wrists and ankles, hoping that would hold him until Danny's cleanup team arrived.

Jackson stepped back inside after loading his car. "We're ready."

"Good," Simon said, tossing Jackson a burner phone. "You, Sport, and Danny use your rental and take the long way around. Edgar and I will go in his truck."

Jackson nodded. "See you in a bit."

Simon saluted him.

CHAPTER FIFTEEN

About half an hour later, Edgar pulled into the parking lot of a seedy motel. Actually, it was an insult to the word seedy to associate it with the place. "You sure about this, Si?"

"Fancy city doc too good for this shit?

"Most third-world countries would condemn this place." Edgar didn't even want to think about how filthy the rooms must be.

Simon rolled his eyes. "Let's go."

They paid for two adjoining rooms, which had actual metal keys. Edgar shuddered when he opened the door. The room smelled like stale smoke and piss, but at least there weren't any mice, roaches, or dead bodies visible.

Jackson, Danny, and Sport arrived a few minutes later, and it was a good thing they texted first. Simon might have shot them if they'd knocked. He was jumpier than Edgar had seen him in a long time.

"Did you drive like a fucking maniac? We thought it'd be another fifteen minutes at least before you showed up," Edgar said.

Sport rolled his eyes. "He always drives like death is nipping at his heels."

"Sometimes it is," Jackson said.

"You really think we should move forward?" Sport asked. Edgar was glad he hadn't needed to be the one to question the validity of this mission.

Simon nodded. "We have to."

"Kingsford is a well-known admiral still on active duty. How long can he stay in hiding?"

"He can't stay out of sight, but he can make sure no one ever connects him to what he's doing."

Edgar could hear the desperation in his voice and he wished he could ease it, but he couldn't let Simon's fears send them all into something they wouldn't walk away from, not if there was another way. "Chances are, since you escaped, he's moved all the evidence he had at The Retreat or destroyed it."

Sport nodded in agreement. "If his endgame really is building forces for a coup, then at least we have a direction. We've known all along there was far more than money at stake here—African pirates, South American drug lords, organized crime in the States—other than bribes that bring in money, something has to connect all those endeavors."

"It fits," Jackson said. "They've got supporters in the CIA, the FBI, the Navy, probably other branches of the military, Congress at least, if not the executive branch."

"I still can't really believe these bastards are planning a fucking coup," Edgar said. Initially, when Simon had told him Danny had been sent to the *Ridgeway* by the CIA, Edgar had figured the bastards who'd sold them out were in some power game, but he'd never thought it was that serious. Of course, Danny and Simon had only recently been able to prove the connections between all the incidents they'd assumed Zenk and Arthurs had orchestrated.

"Then let's quit wasting time," Jackson said.

Danny frowned. "I don't like how there's no one there." Before he could say more, his phone rang. "It's Darrow," he said as he accepted the call.

Edgar sat down and let his head drop into his hands. He hadn't really slept in far too long and he was running on caffeine and adrenaline. Thinking about Kingsford amassing an army had his head pounding. He was glad he hadn't eaten recently, because he doubted food would've stayed down. Bits of Danny's conversation came to him as Danny paced the room.

"Nothing. But…"

"Yeah they might."

"We will. Six hours."

"We will. Thanks."

"What did he say?" Simon asked after Danny ended the call.

"Still no sign of movement at The Retreat."

"Does he think we should check it out?" Sport asked.

Edgar hated this. Everything about it felt wrong. "What does your gut tell you, Si? Do you really believe this is the right thing to do or do you just want it to be?"

Simon shook his head. "It doesn't matter. Right or wrong, we can't let this lead go."

"The fuck we can't," Edgar said, pissed that Simon couldn't see his thinking was compromised on this one.

"If we all get killed, then who the fuck is going to report our findings anyway?" Danny asked. The fact that Danny was nervous about charging in only added to Edgar's apprehension.

Simon picked up a glass and threw it. It smashed against the far wall, and for a few seconds, no one spoke. "I don't fucking know, okay? I don't know anything except that whether any of the rest of you fucking care or not, I'm going to find the man who sent me and my crew out to die, the man who ruined my career, my life. I just wanted a ship. I worked hard to get there, and they took that from me."

Danny laid a hand on Simon's shoulder, but he shook it off.

"You're too close to this," he said. "From now on, I'm running this mission."

"Like you're not compromised by this, like you don't—"

"Simon, for once, you're going to fucking listen to me."

Simon shoved Danny away and walked across the room.

Edgar was done with them all. "Maybe instead of walking into a trap, we can just all beat the shit out of each other and save those bastards the time." He stomped into the adjoining room and slammed the thin door. It was a miracle it didn't fall of the hinges. "Fucking assholes," he muttered.

Like you're any easier to deal with. Did his conscience really need to speak in Si's voice?

I'm not that *fucking bad.*

You have your days.

He huffed. He was dog-tired and he wanted to lie down, but the comforter on the bed was stained with something he hoped wasn't blood. A dip in the middle of the mattress indicated that the springs were shot, not that they'd likely been all that strong to start with. No thanks. He'd just stand. He paced back and forth, trying to block out the voices still shouting at each other in the next room, not easy to do when the walls might as well have been nonexistent.

He should have brought some earplugs. Just when he was considering jumping out the window because he couldn't take it anymore, Simon burst into the room. Anger and fear made him look feral, not at all the smooth, seductive man he usually pretended to be. Simon slammed the door and surprisingly, it survived the treatment once again.

"I've had it," Simon announced.

"*You've* had it?"

"Fucking right, I have. I'm so fucking done with arguing."

"So there's still no consensus?" Edgar asked.

"We're going in an hour before dawn."

Simon brushed a hand over his hair, leaving it standing on end. Si's hair was famous for never being out of place, but apparently the tension of the day was too much even for whatever hair magic he possessed. Simon looked out into the night through the huge hole in the curtain.

Edgar stepped closer and fixed his hair. "We really picked a classy place, huh?"

Si laughed, the sound bitter. "Yeah, we did."

"I want to fuck you, but the bed's too sketchy."

Simon's breath caught. "What?"

Edgar smiled, loving that he'd caught Si off guard. "You acting like an ass has no effect on my desire for you."

Simon's eyes lit up. "Good."

"Damn right, since you're an ass most of the

time."

"If it turns you on, I'll be one all the fucking time."

"I wouldn't go that far."

"Are you sure?" Simon dropped his hand to Edgar's cock. "This says differently."

"I might not like your attitude, but when you burst in that door, all wild and breathing hard, you looked like you needed to be put up against the wall."

"So do it. The walls have to be cleaner than the bed."

Edgar glanced around the room. He wasn't so sure. What were those smudges? Fuck it, he'd take the risk. He backed Simon up until he thunked against the peeling paint.

Simon dropped his head back and laughed. "I fucking love you like this."

"You'd better, because with your attitude, I'm going to be like this a lot."

Simon tilted his hips so he could rub against Edgar's crotch. "Horny?"

"Pissed off and wanting to take it out on your ass."

***

Edgar kissed Simon before he could make a sassy comeback, but he didn't care. He didn't need a comeback with Edgar. That might be his best defense with most people, but Edgar saw through everything he tried. He saw all that was raw and hurting in Simon, yet he didn't push him away. Even when Edgar said he was done with Simon's crap, Edgar took him in anyway.

Edgar plundered his mouth, and Simon fucking

loved the way he was staking his claim. No matter what he'd said to Edgar, he knew he couldn't go back to taking the types of missions he was used to. He'd been able to stomach doing whatever was necessary to meet his objectives because he'd been dead inside for years. The men he'd fucked had given him a release of tension but never anything more. Nothing had really touched him below the surface until Edgar. Just a simple caress from him was better than any of the mindless rough sex Simon had treated himself to on the job.

Edgar undid Simon's cargo pants as Simon did the same for him. Then Edgar pushed Simon's hands away so he could work both their cocks. Simon thrust into his grip, groaning at the feel of his cock pressed to Edgar's. Edgar let go and slid his hands into the waistband of Si's pants. Gripping Simon's ass, Edgar yanked them together so their cocks were trapped between them. Edgar took Si's hands in his, pulled his arms up, and pressed them against he wall. Simon could've broken free if he wanted, but he had no desire to get away from Edgar. No matter how angry Edgar was, no matter how hurt he looked, Simon had to stay and face it. He needed this man more than he'd ever needed anything.

Edgar thrust against him, rubbing their cocks together. Simon met each of his thrusts. God, it felt good. He could come like that. Easily. Too easily. Edgar stole all his control. "More."

"I'll give you more." Edgar thrust harder.

"Need you to fuck me."

"You love that, don't you, having my cock up your ass?"

More than anything. "God yes."

Edgar nipped at Simon's throat, then rested his head on Si's shoulder. "Fuck."

Simon tensed. "What's wrong?"

"The fucking condoms are in the bag in the other room."

He started to step away but Simon grabbed his arm and tugged him back. He wanted Edgar bare. He needed to share that intimacy with him, and he didn't want to think whether that was stupid or not. "Don't go."

Edgar frowned. "It will just take a sec. I'll be right back."

"I don't want you to use one."

Edgar studied him. "Si…"

"I'm clean. I swear." He was suddenly desperate to convince Edgar. He'd never wanted that with anyone. It was one of the few things he'd always been careful about. "I know you think I fuck everyone in sight, but I don't, not really. I got tested before my last mission and I haven't been with anyone since then except you. If you say you're clean, then I trust you."

"I'm careful. Very careful."

"Then fuck me, Edgar. I want to feel the heat of your cock in my ass. I want you to fill me up with cum."

His eyes widened. "Holy shit, Simon. I—"

Simon put a finger on his lip. "Edgar, you're going to fuck me until I forget the danger, forget Kingsford, forget everything but you."

Simon could see the heat in Edgar's eyes, but the tension in his body told Simon he was still fighting the inevitable. "You're wounded."

"I'll be fine."

"God, Si, you make me stupid, and that's not something I can afford to be with you dragging me back into the field."

Edgar was right and Simon knew it, but he didn't care. For the next few minutes, nothing existed but the two of them. "You can be as stupid as you like just as long as you put your dick in my ass."

***

Edgar growled as he lifted Simon and carried him into the bathroom. The counter there was cracked but less shudder-inducing than the bed. He set Si on his feet. "Don't fucking move."

Was he really going to do this? Was he going to fuck Simon with the others in the next room? Fuck yes, he was, and he intended to make Simon scream. Edgar pulled his shirt off and laid it on the counter. As he started to lift Simon up to sit on the counter, he froze. "Si, this isn't going to work. We don't have lube either."

"I'll fix that." Simon dropped to his knees and rubbed his face against Edgar's cock. Then he sucked it sloppily, letting spit run down the shaft.

"Si, there's lube in my bag if you just let me…"

Simon pulled off his cock long enough to say. "No. You're staying right here.

"Si, I don't want to hurt you, I…" Simon swallowed Edgar's cock again. "Fuck!" He'd never felt anything like the sensation of being down Simon's throat. All thought of speaking or protesting what was happening vanished.

He was going to do this. He was going to fuck

Simon bareback with spit for lube against a bathroom counter than might or might not hold him up, in a motel that made some of the third-world hovels he'd been in look like palaces. Then they were going on what might amount to a suicide run. Two days ago he'd just been living his boring life as a family doc in the city.

What the fuck happened?

Simon.

Simon always happens just when I get comfortable.

And you fucking love it.

Yeah. I do.

Si licked him, teasing before taking him down again.

"Jesus, Si. I can't—"

Simon swallowed his cock until his lips brushed Edgar's pubic bone. "Holy fuck! I'm going to come if you don't stop that!"

Simon pulled off and smiled up at him.

The blissed-out expression on his face did something crazy to Edgar. "Marry me."

"I thought you'd never ask," Simon responded, voice gone dreamy. Then he ruined it by cracking up. "I'm damn good with my mouth, aren't I? Lots of guys have that reaction."

His words hit Edgar like a punch. He pushed Simon away and stepped back.

Simon gaped at him. "What the hell are you upset for?" Before Edgar responded, Simon's expression changed to one of shock. "Fucking hell, you weren't kidding, were you?"

"Yes. No." The words had just come out, but not

because of Simon's wicked mouth. "What if I were?"

"You… Edgar I can't think about that until after… Until we know what we're up against." Simon stood and wrapped a hand around the back of Edgar's neck pulling him down until their lips nearly touched. "I do love you, though, even if I am a fucked-up mess."

"You are that and more, but aren't we all?"

Simon nibbled Edgar's earlobe. "Please say you're still going to fuck me."

"Hell yes, I'm going to fuck you." That train left the station when Si got on his knees. "Turn around and brace yourself."

Simon took hold of the counter, and Edgar shoved his pants down to his ankles.

"If this hurts too much, you better fucking tell me. And you better warn me if we're tearing your wound open again."

"I'm not stopping you, Edgar. Not for any fucking thing. Nothing you do could really hurt me unless you walked away."

"I'm never walking away from you, Si. I think we've learned that doesn't work."

"Damn right it doesn't and you better—oh my fucking God!"

Edgar pushed the tip of his spit-slicked cock against Si's ass.

"Fuck that feels good. I've never barebacked with anyone."

A wave of possessiveness hit Edgar so hard his knees buckled. "And you won't ever do this with anyone else, you got that? Your ass is mine now."

"Yes! Fuck, yes!"

Edgar pushed in farther. Simon whimpered. "That's right. Open for me, Si."

Simon pushed back, trying to take him deeper. Edgar squeezed his hips, refusing to let him take control. "I'm in charge right now. Your job is to take it."

Simon glanced over his shoulder. "Don't stop. Please. I'll beg. I'll—"

Simon's words ended with a strangled sound when Edgar drove deep.

"You feel good, Si, so hot and tight around my cock."

Simon whined and struggled against his hold. "Fuck me!"

"I am fucking you."

"No, you're standing still."

Edgar slapped his ass, and Simon purred. "Figures you'd like that."

"What the fuck does that—?"

Edgar drove in more. "You love being filled up with my cock, don't you?"

"Fuck yes! This is… I've never…"

Edgar pulled out all the way, then drove hard, holding still when he was buried to the balls.

Simon squirmed under him. "Please. Edgar, please. I'll do anything. I—"

Edgar used slow, careful strokes. He was torturing himself as much as Simon, but he didn't care. He loved making Simon beg. He leaned over Simon's back and whispered in his ear. "Am I hurting you?"

"No. Yes. God, Edgar, I told you I don't mind when it hurts. I don't care if you split me in two. I want to feel what you've done to my ass for as long as this mission lasts."

"Fuck!" Why was that so goddamned hot? Edgar increased his pace until he was riding Simon hard and Simon was cursing and shouting and driving back against him, desperate for more. "That's right. Take it all, Si. Take everything you want."

Simon started jacking himself. Edgar wanted to do it for him, but his head was swimming. He couldn't think about anything but driving his dick into Simon's ass.

"Si. Si. I'm… Oh fuck, I'm…" His orgasm hit so hard he saw stars. He bucked against Simon as he shot deep in his ass, loving how his cum made the strokes easier.

CHAPTER SIXTEEN

Simon couldn't catch his breath. He was burning up from the inside out and yet it was the best feeling in the world. He could feel Edgar coming inside him. That flood of heat was all it took to send him over. He worked his cock faster and faster as his balls drew up and he started to come. The sensation was so sharp it was both pain and relief. His arms slipped and he lay on the counter, though he wondered if he would ooze off and pool on the floor, boneless.

Edgar started to raise off him.

Simon reached behind him, straining to grab hold and stop him. "No."

"Si, are you okay?"

"Yeah, just give me a minute." The area around his side burned. He didn't feel any wetness there so probably the stitches hadn't split. His ass was going to hurt like hell, but that was as much pleasure as pain. The real reason he didn't want Edgar to move was because he wanted time to enjoy having him as close as he could possibly be.

Edgar exhaled loudly and braced himself against the counter, hands on either side of Si. "It's going to hurt when I pull out, isn't it?"

"Yeah." It was easier to let him think that was Simon's only concern.

"Get ready then. My legs are cramping up. I've

got to move."

Simon nodded.

"Okay. One, two—" He pulled back and Simon gasped.

"Fuckity fucking fuck!"

Edgar laughed. "Yeah. I can imagine."

Simon could feel Edgar's cum running down his leg. God, that felt almost good enough to make his cock rise again. He didn't think he was ever going to move.

He watched Edgar turn on the sink, pick up a washcloth, examine it and then wet it. "Let me wipe you off. I think these are clean enough."

"I fucking love the mess of this, knowing that's your cum running from my ass. It's... hot."

Edgar chuckled. "It's kind of hot knowing I did that to you."

"Is it now?"

Simon jerked away when Edgar placed the washcloth against him. "That's fucking cold!"

"I don't think we have hot water in here."

Simon shouldn't have been surprised.

"Let me see your wound," Edgar said after he'd cleaned Simon's ass and thighs.

Simon tried to stand, but he had to grab the counter when the room tilted. "Wow! I've never been fucked so hard I couldn't stand up afterward."

"God, Si. Are you okay?"

Simon laughed. "I think you literally blew my fucking mind."

Edgar ignored him and bent to examine his wound. "It's red, but I think you'll do."

"I'll more than do. I feel like I'm fucking flying.

Your dick is better than Percocet."

"Fucking hell, don't tell Danny that or I'll never hear the end of it."

Simon just grinned at him.

"You do know we've got to go back over there and work out the rest of our plan," Edgar said as he held Simon's clothes out to him.

"Yeah, I'm just trying to ignore it."

Edgar stood and reached for his pants. "Come on."

Simon groaned. "I want to stay here and enjoy it. Of course, that would be easier if the bed didn't look like bedbugs might be the nicest thing living on it."

They dressed in silence. Edgar took a step toward the door, but Simon seized his arm. "I love you. No matter what happens, I need you to remember that."

"Si, I love you too, and you goddamn better act like you've got something to live for today."

"I do. More than I have in a long time."

When they stepped back into the other room, Danny whistled.

Jackson shook his head. "If anyone's looking for us, they sure as hell know where we are now." He looked at Edgar. "What the fuck did you do to him?"

"Nothing he didn't deserve."

"Exactly what I needed," Simon said with a smirk. "Are you assholes ready to finalize this?"

"How can we be sure our intel is legit?" Edgar asked.

"Reed's doing the observation of the house," Sport said. "He was on our team. He still is, actually, but he's in Little Creek now as an instructor."

Edgar nodded. He couldn't argue with their

confidence in their former teammate. When you worked that closely with a man, you really got to know him. "And the other contacts?"

Simon glanced at Danny.

"I trust them."

"Okay, then," Simon said. "Let's finalize this."

***

A few hours later, they had as solid a plan as they could make. Sport and Jackson would approach from the woods surrounding the house on the north side. Danny, Simon, and Edgar would move in from the water, playing the part of drunken revelers taking their boat out until they were given the all clear by Sport and Jackson. Darrow, Sport's SAIC would position himself nearby and take over satellite surveillance.

Jackson and Sport gathered their gear and headed out, wanting to get in place before the others procured a boat. Edgar paced while Simon and Danny argued over the last details. He glanced at the door to the adjoining room, wishing he could drag Simon back there. Edgar had caught Simon watching him more than once, looking like he wanted to devour him, and Edgar knew he was always hyped up with sexual energy before a mission.

Danny still didn't like how things felt and the tension in the room was so thick, Edgar could hardly breathe. Danny started cleaning his gun for the fourth or fifth time that night, a sure sign he was agitated. Edgar peeked through the ratty curtains, scanning the parking lot for anyone who might be watching them, but all he saw were empty cars and a stray cat.

"Edgar, come on." Simon tugged him toward the

adjoining room.

He'd kept his hands off Simon, knowing Simon needed to focus on making a plan, but if he wanted to pass the last bit of time they had fucking, Edgar wasn't about to say no.

Simon shut the door, closing Danny out, though not really giving them privacy.

"I need to talk to you," Simon said.

Edgar studied him, worried by the apprehension in his eyes. "I take it that's not a euphemism."

Simon shook his head.

Several seconds passed in silence. "Talk," Edgar said. Simon was usually more straightforward that this.

"I know I begged you to come with me," Simon said. "But you're staying here."

"Staying here? What the fuck?"

"Darrow will contact you if we need you, but you're too much of a distraction for me."

Edgar closed his eyes and fought the rage pulsing through him. Punching Simon wouldn't help, though it would feel really damn good. "You are not fucking leaving me behind. I've saved your ass in the field plenty of times, and I'll do it again if you need me, or if any of the rest of them need me. That's what I'm trained for and that's what I'm going to do."

"Edgar—"

"Fuck! The whole 'whatever happens just know I love you'. You'd already planned to leave me then." Edgar felt sick. Edgar might not have wanted to go back into the field, but he'd be damned if Simon thought he could order him around.

"I need you safe. I can't go out there if you…"

Simon's voice broke and his eyes shone with tears. Edgar had to look away and get himself under control. He had no idea if the tears were real or it was more of the famed Simon McLeod manipulation techniques.

"Si, this is my fight too. You can't shut me out. They found us at my cabin. They could find me here. There's no such thing as a safe place to hide."

Simon shook his head. "You'll be safe here."

"What the fuck makes you say that?" There was something he wasn't getting, something Simon hadn't told him.

"Darrow's making sure of it."

"What the fuck, Si? You've brought him in as a babysitter? For me?" He squeezed his hands into fists. *Don't hit him. Don't hit him.* He shoved at Simon's chest and walked across the room, needing some distance. He leaned on the bathroom doorframe, trying to breathe.

"Look, I know you—"

"You brought me out here and now you think I'm just going to sit on my ass? Fuck no. I'm in this all the way."

"You're staying here. That's an order."

A fucking order? Oh hell no. "So that's what this has come down to?"

"You're acting like a stubborn dick, so yes." Simon kept his voice steady, controlled, but Edgar could see the fear and tension vibrating through him. He wanted to put the fucking bastard in his place and comfort him at the same time. *This relationship is so fucked up.* "You seem to be forgetting that I'm not on your ship anymore. You're not my captain, and you don't get to give me orders just because I don't like your insane-as-fuck plan."

Simon took a step back. The pain in his eyes seemed so real, but Edgar had seen him make that play before. Those puppy eyes weren't going to get fuck-all for Si no matter how blue they were, no matter how much Edgar wanted to fall into them like he would a tropical sea.

"You're not on my team?" Simon asked as if Edgar had said he didn't love him anymore rather than that he didn't take orders from him.

Edgar chose to ignore the significance of that, because otherwise he'd be under Simon's spell in no time.

"I got out of that life, remember? But I'm not sure you're ever going to stop living on the edge."

Simon frowned. Edgar hated how he no longer looked in control. He looked young and desperate, but Edgar wouldn't give in.

"I couldn't just sit on my ass," Simon protested. "I have to have—"

"Danger. Near-death experiences."

"Fine. I'm a fucking adrenaline junkie. I thrive on fear. Is that so wrong?"

It is when I don't know if you're dead or alive for months at a time. "It's who you are, but I can't be a part of it."

"But I need you."

Then why are you pushing me away? "You have to make choices."

"Are you really happy with your life like it is?"

Fuck no. But mostly because Simon wasn't there, not because he needed to risk his life every fucking

175

day.

"Don't you want to be doing more?"

"I do plenty."

Simon glared at him. "Fine."

Edgar forced himself to look away from the pain in Simon's eyes. He wasn't staying in the fucking hotel being watched over by some elusive contact of Si's. As to how much of Si's act he bought into and what they would be doing after this mission, he wasn't sure, but right now they needed to gear up and get the fuck out of there.

He reached for his sidearm and settled it into his holster. Then he reached for his backup, but Simon stepped closer, leaning down and kissing his neck.

"Si. This isn't the time."

"Sure it is." Si slid a hand across his chest and then brushed it over Edgar's crotch. His fucking traitorous cock reacted, swelling under Simon's touch. Si brushed his lips over Edgar's neck. "I love you."

Edgar sighed but before he could reply, Simon grabbed his pistol from his holster with one hand while knocking the other gun off the table where Edgar couldn't reach it.

"What the fuck are you doing?" Edgar's heart pounded as he stared into the barrel of his own pistol, which Si had trained on him. He had a sickening thought. "Oh God, Si. You're not the one feeding Kingsford's men information, are you?" Edgar fought the roiling of his stomach. If Simon had betrayed them, he hoped to God Si would just shoot him then and there, because he was never going to recover from that.

Simon's eyes widened and he stumbled, losing his aim for a second. "No! Fuck no! Edgar, how could you think—?"

"You're holding a fucking gun on me, that's how."

"I just need you to listen. To accept that you can't come with me."

"Simon, put the goddamn gun down."

Simon shook his head. "I'm protecting you." His stance was wide and he kept glancing to the door, the window. He looked wild, like a caged animal. This mission had really fucked him up. He had no business in the field like this.

"Danny!" Edgar called.

Simon shook his head. "He won't interfere. He promised me."

"You're both fucking nuts."

"He knows I can't think with you there. I thought I could convince you, but you wouldn't listen and—"

Simon's voice broke. He was near panic. Edgar might be able to overpower him, but one of them also might get seriously hurt. Simon was unpredictable when he *wasn't* half crazed.

"You seriously thought I'd just roll over and do your bidding because you're some superstar operative and I'm just what—a prop?"

"No, I love you."

"And you swore you'd never lie to me about that, never use desire to manipulate me." That hurt the worst, far more than Simon's crazy ideas of protecting him, more even than Si holding a fucking gun on him.

"I'm sorry. I know you're probably going to hate

me, but at least you'll be alive."

"Simon, don't do this. Let me be there for you. Let me be there to put you together after this. Please."

Simon shook his head. "I can't." He pulled out a pair of cuffs and snapped one around Edgar's wrists and the other around the bedframe. Edgar should have fought him, but he was too stunned, too disbelieving that this was really happening. He also had a universal handcuff key in his pocket. Thank God habits ingrained from his spec-op days never seemed to go away.

"You're going to leave me here like this and walk into God knows what kind of trap. What if this is the last I see of you?"

Simon didn't look at him. He laid Edgar's gun down on the table, just barely out of his reach and then picked up his backup weapon and put it there as well. "I love you, Edgar, even if you don't believe me."

"You really know how to show it, leaving me cuffed and defenseless."

"You'll be out of that in no time."

True, but that wasn't the point. "Which proves I'm not fucking helpless. I can be an asset out there."

Simon kept his gaze fixed toward the door to the next room. "I know, but, Edgar…" Simon wiped at his eyes. Was he fucking crying? He was really losing it, which meant he needed Edgar by his side more than ever. Once Simon left, Edgar would free himself and go after him. Did Simon really think he'd stay there waiting like a fucking pet?

Simon left, and Edgar stared at the door he'd closed between them. Why the fuck did he have to love a man as fucked-up as Simon? Why couldn't he hate him when he ought to?

Because you know how hurt he is. You understand the desperation that would make him do this.

He fucking cuffed me to a bed. He fucking decided for me that I can't be on the mission he *dragged me into.* Edgar kicked at the bed and it slid across the floor, pulling him with it. "Fucking son of a bitch!"

Simon couldn't hear him, though. Edgar had heard his truck—his own fucking truck—speed out of the parking lot. Danny must've had it running before Simon had walked away.

Where was Darrow? Would he really come for Edgar if he deemed it necessary? He wasn't going to find him there, because Edgar wouldn't be there more than a few minutes. He twisted to reach his left hand into his right front pocket where he always kept a key.

Lock him up with his own cuffs, would he? Simon would pay and so would fucking Danny, but right now, Edgar needed to worry about saving their sorry asses first.

CHAPTER SEVENTEEN

Simon realized he'd made a mistake by the time he and Danny had helped themselves to a boat. "Edgar's going to hate me."

"Did you expect otherwise?" Danny had told him to tell Edgar his concerns but not to push. Of course he hadn't listened, which Danny would have known. What had Simon expected, that Edgar would be okay with his high-handedness, that he'd jump to follow Simon's command? Edgar had never hesitated to question him even during the time they both served on the *Ridgeway*. Simon's interactions with Edgar were different than with most officers because of his position as the senior medical officer. Edgar had always forced Si to think through some of his rasher notions.

Simon had crossed a line today. Had he ruined their chances for a future? Maybe, but it didn't matter. He had to think about now. There might not be a tomorrow. Still, he couldn't stop thinking of the anger and, worse, the hurt in Edgar's eyes as Simon had left him. He wasn't going to be able to concentrate on the mission no matter where Edgar was. He knew that now. Why had he ever brought him here?

Because you need him. Once you saw him, you couldn't just disappear again.

For weeks, Simon had dreamed of the *Ridgeway* almost every night. He'd initially let Edgar stay on board, and when he'd ordered him to leave, Edgar had defied him. Even after saving Simon's life, Edgar refused to walk. Their captors/rescuers had dragged Edgar away screaming. He'd had to be sedated before they could get him on a plane back to the States.

"Danny, are you sure Darrow is trustworthy?"

"I'm as sure of him as I am of Sport. Well, I haven't slept with him, but—"

"I'm serious. I left Edgar there defenseless, except for Darrow watching over him."

Danny snorted. "You know Edgar's out of those cuffs by now and probably hunting us down."

Simon swallowed against the nausea that rose, thinking of Edgar out there on his own. "That really makes me feel better."

"Did you actually think leaving him behind would help?" Danny asked.

"I don't want to be responsible for him getting killed." Simon had let Edgar sail into a trap with him on the *Ridgeway*. He wasn't going to do that again.

"I get that. But if I tried that fucking shit with Sport—"

"He would put a bullet in you."

Danny nodded.

Simon tried to focus on getting their weapons loaded into the boat, but his mind was whirling. "God, I hope we live through this."

"You'll have to confront Edgar then. It might be easier to be dead."

Simon flipped him off as he stepped into the rickety craft, praying it would hold them. He wondered if the owner had insurance. He might get a better boat out of it if he did.

Danny opened a bottle of cheap-ass whiskey and sloshed some on each of them. Then he pulled on a hat to make himself less recognizable. Simon did the same. They laid a pair of night-vision goggles in the bottom of the boat. Those would be for later if they made it to shore.

Danny rowed for a bit. When they got closer to Kingsford's cabin, Simon started talking loudly, saying shit about some women they'd supposedly given their numbers to. Danny laughed and Si saluted him with the bottle.

"See anything?" he asked Danny quietly while pretending to drink.

"Nope, not a damn thing," Danny answered, his voice loud.

"Yeah, I bet we won't get anything from them either." Simon was almost shouting. While drunken assholes annoyed everyone, no one paid close attention to them.

A light flashed in the woods, Jackson or Sport giving the all clear. Time to stop the game and get serious.

Danny rowed up to the shore. They tied the boat and circled around the house to meet the others. Danny surveyed the place with the goggles. "I don't see anything, but something feels wrong."

Simon felt it too. It was too quiet.

Jackson inclined his head toward the front door of the house once they'd all gathered. "Assuming we can't disable the alarm, we'll have about ten minutes before the police arrive. As to anyone else who'll

Silvia Violet

respond… we've got no idea. Based on what we've seen, there's a door with its own alarm keypad that likely leads to the basement. We should blow it to get in there fast."

Calm descended over Simon, as it always did at this point in a mission. He'd feared he wouldn't be able to reach that otherworldly state, so he welcomed it. In that mode of hyperconcentration, he could ignore fear, pain, and logic. "You and Sport clear the house; Danny and I will go for the door."

They moved in. When they were within a few feet of the back door, Simon held up his hand, signaling the others to stay back and cover him. He tried the door. You never knew when someone would leave a door open. Why break in if you could walk in? No luck. He picked the lock in seconds. Then he tried the best combos he could think of on the alarm pad. No go.

Danny was already laying a strip of explosives along the reinforced door they hoped hid what they were looking for. Simon could hear Sport and Jackson moving through the house. They hadn't seen anyone yet, but they also hadn't found anything of interest.

There were no personal touches in the house and it was immaculately clean. Simon's gut was still telling him things weren't right when Danny signaled that he was ready and they moved to the side of the door. Just before Danny pressed the detonator, Simon imagined them getting caught setting off explosives in an innocent admiral's house. What if they were wrong? He didn't think even Danny's contacts could save them from that goatfuck. But his certainty of

Kingsford's guilt was at least as strong as his feeling that something wasn't as it seemed.

Bang! The door swung in, dangling from one hinge, and Simon and Danny charged through, weapons drawn. They shone their flashlights down the stairs, but all they could see was what looked like lab equipment. When they reached the bottom step, Danny flicked on a light switch. Simon sucked in his breath. "Holy fuck!"

"Main floor is clear!" Jackson called down the stairs.

"One of you needs to come see this," Danny said. Simon nodded as if they could see him.

"Go," he heard Jackson say. "My leg's no good on stairs. I'll be lookout."

Simon had yet to move. He was staring at the room, trying to take it in. Danny was already riffling through papers and opening a laptop that sat on a desk by a chair where someone—a patient? A victim?—would sit. The room looked like the lair of a mad scientist.

"He's not just trying to build an army; he's experimenting with how to make them stronger."

"This is something out of a fucking movie," Sport said as he worked his way around the room.

Simon still couldn't speak. There were files with subjects—people—and lists of drugs they'd been given and their reaction.

"Fuck me," Danny said.

"What did you find?"

"Kingsford's been running tests on his mercs. Physical tests, but not just to see how fit they are. He's trying to develop a cocktail of drugs and herbs that will make them stronger and more resilient."

"Like a fucking supersoldier?" Sport asked. "So he's not just a murdering bastard, he's fucking nuts."

"I think so." Danny turned the laptop so Simon and Jackson could see what he was reading, but as he did so, his phone rang. "Darrow," he said when he glanced at it.

An explosion rocked the building before he could answer it.

"At least four men out there!" Jackson called.

Where the fuck had the attack come from? Simon wondered as he and the others raced for the stairs.

***

Edgar had the cuffs unlocked in no time. "Fucking Simon," he muttered as he placed his gun back in his shoulder holster. He wondered if the keys to Danny's car were around or not. He'd hotwire it if he needed to.

If they all survived this day, what the fuck was he going to do about his former captain who'd become his lover and then used even that connection to get what he wanted? *Fucking little shit.*

Simon was damn lucky Edgar understood that Simon's world revolved around protecting people. While Edgar had served on the *Ridgeway*, Simon had demonstrated again and again that he felt completely accountable for the lives of all the men and women serving under him. If there was anything he could do to lessen the dangers his crew faced, he would do it. He would rather take any level of risk on himself than expose another person to it. That was just how he was wired. But goddamm, Edgar was pissed as fuck that Simon had walked away from him, and the next time he saw Simon, he intended to punch him in his charming face.

Edgar froze. Someone was at the door. Instead of holstering his backup pistol, he kept it out and crept toward the door, positioning himself so he'd be behind it when whoever was out there jimmied the flimsy lock.

"Edgar?" a man's voice called.

"Who's there?" The door swung open and Edgar took cover but the man stepped into the room with his hands up.

"I'm Clark Darrow, Special Agent in Charge, Washington Field Office, Criminal Division."

Edgar assessed him, still wary. "Show me some ID."

"Danny warned me you'd be as likely to shoot me as listen." The man pulled out his badge and opened it for Edgar. It looked all right, but credentials, like anything else, could be faked.

"I'm here as a friend," Darrow said. "I understand why you'd be suspicious. But I've been working with Danny and Simon for years, and I'm on your side. I have no more reason to trust you than you do to trust me."

Edgar nodded. That was true, although the idea that Edgar himself would be suspect made him bristle. "I've known Simon a hell of a lot longer than you have, and I was in South America—"

Darrow held up his hand. "You don't need to recite your qualifications to me. Someone we all thought was loyal is selling us out. So I've got reason to be jumpy too."

"You know who it is?"

Darrow nodded. "I'll explain once we're in the car. We've got to move now. There were men approaching The Retreat, and I can't get Danny to answer his fucking phone."

Edgar was out the door before Darrow finished his sentence. He gestured to the black SUV that screamed government agent.

"You driving?"

"Yes, they know we're coming anyway."

They entered the vehicle, and Darrow sped out of the parking lot.

"Who?" Edgar asked, trying to ignore the nausea tightening his throat.

Darrow glanced at him, and Edgar noted hesitation on his face. "Just fucking say it."

"Reed Devereaux."

Oh fuck no. "This will gut Jackson and Sport. Their fucking teammate?"

"None of the intelligence from Reed, not even the footage he hooked me into, showed anyone at that goddamn cabin. So when Danny told me you found someone watching your lake house, I decided to poke around. I called in a favor, and when I got visuals, there they were, at least six men watching Kingsford's place. They've probably been there the whole fucking time."

"And Reed covered it all up." Edgar slammed his hand down on the console. "How? His own teammate was killed by these people. What kind of fucking bastard does this?"

Darrow shook his head. "An evil one."

"But why?"

"Money most likely, maybe other promises from

Kingsford."

"Where is he now?" Edgar asked.

"He disappeared after I broke contact with him. I've got men looking for him."

"What about Derrick? Danny still thinks we can trust him, but—"

Darrow blew out an exasperated breath. "Gone. No one's seen him in two days. And we don't know a damn thing. He may have run. He may have been killed. He may be with those fuckers right now, planning how to take us all out."

"Fuck!" This was getting worse by the second.

"We've also lost contact with the safe house where his wife and children were. Reed may have lied to us about their safety too."

"Holy fuck." If Derrick's family was compromised or… worse. There was no telling what he would do.

"What about Addy?" Edgar didn't even want to think about how Jackson would react if something happened to him. He wouldn't stop until every person who'd ever so much as held a door open for Kingsford was dead. Edgar was certain of that, because if they killed Simon…

"Addy's fine. He's with one of the few men I trust right now."

"What about Derrick's family? What can be done?"

"I hope to God they're alive, but I've got to take on one crisis at a time."

Darrow drove like a maniac while continuing to dial Danny's number. Edgar held on and didn't say another word until they turned onto a path barely wide enough for the car.

When it narrowed more, Darrow stopped the car and they both got out. Darrow popped the trunk, tossed Edgar a semiautomatic weapon, and then armed himself.

Darrow punched at his phone again. "Fuck! Why won't Danny answer?"

An explosion followed by a rain of gunfire broke the peace of the night. Darrow tossed Edgar a pair of night-vision goggles. Then they ran toward the flashes they could see through the trees.

They positioned themselves at the edge of the clearing where the house stood and started taking out their opponents. Darrow brought down a man with a grenade launcher, and Edgar shot two of the men who were shooting at the figures escaping from the building.

A figure exited the cabin, Sport, if Edgar had to guess based on size and build. One of Kingsford's men whistled and the rest of them scattered, melting into the woods. Edgar fired at them to cover Sport's escape.

Then an explosion lit up the night. It was a direct hit on the house. Where were the others? Had they gotten out? He couldn't see anything but smoke and fire.

"Are they fucking bombing the place?" Darrow asked.

"Simon!" Edgar screamed. Darrow grabbed for him, but he tore free and ran toward the cabin. Someone tackled him and he fought them. "Simon! He's in there! I have to get him out!"

"No, no, he's not. They took him."

"What? No! He can't. If they—"

"We're going to get him back, Edgar. I swear to you. I will save him or die trying." Danny rolled off Edgar and stood up. Edgar tried to follow him, but his legs didn't seem to work. He was going to lose it just like he had in the jungle.

Jackson appeared from the far side of the house. "Did you see Simon?" Edgar asked.

"No." Jackson shook his head like it was still ringing from the blast. Edgar's was too and Jackson been much closer. "I fought my way free, but Simon was unconscious. They headed west. That's all I know."

"We've got to get out of here and regroup," Darrow said.

"No, we have to find him now before…" Edgar's eyes stung. He was not going to fucking cry.

"Kingsford's men are all over these woods. We've got to get to the car and get out," Darrow insisted.

"He's right," Danny said. He tugged on Edgar's arm, helping him up.

"I can't leave him."

Sport motioned for Danny and the rest to head on. "I swear to you we will find him. We won't stop until we do, but going after them now is not the answer. We're outnumbered. We've got to regroup."

"But we have no idea where they're taking him."

"We'll figure that out, but we need to be alive to do it."

They didn't run into anybody as they made their way back to Darrow's car. They were all too stunned to speak as he drove them to the spot where Danny had left Edgar's truck. It was undamaged.

"Sport, you and Jackson take Edgar with you and pick up Jackson's rental. I need some time with Darrow to figure out our next step."

Edgar allowed Sport to lead him to the truck and basically shove him in; nothing seemed real at that moment. He felt empty inside. What if Simon… No. They would find him. Alive. They had to. Edgar couldn't let himself think of any other possibility.

CHAPTER EIGHTEEN

"I put a tracker in his phone," Danny said as soon as he and Darrow were alone. "I didn't want to say anything in front of Edgar in case they've taken his phone or it's not working, but we should be able to ping his location."

Before Danny finished talking, Darrow was making a call. Danny listened as he gave instructions for Simon's tracker to be activated.

As soon as he hung up, he glanced at Danny. "So what did you find?"

"I'm not even sure I believe what I saw."

Darrow whistled. "That bad?"

"They're working on a drug cocktail to improve strength and speed. The fucking bastard thinks he's going to make the perfect soldier."

"So he *is* building an army?"

"Yeah. It was fucking creepy as hell in there. He's experimenting on people and… it hadn't gone well for all of them."

"Considering the things you've seen, if you found it creepy, then I don't even want to imagine it."

Danny wished he didn't have to. "There wasn't much there, though. If I had to guess, I'd say they've moved somewhere bigger and expanded."

"Fuck, where are they getting the people they're testing shit on?"

Silvia Violet

Danny shrugged. "They might be volunteers or prisoners or God knows who. But what if it works? Think of the implications."

Danny saw Darrow's hands tighten on the wheel. "I think this needs to go all the way up the food chain."

Danny sighed. He hadn't contacted the director of their cadre of shadow agents within the already shadowy CIA since he'd needed her best sniper to back him up with Senator Zenk. "You're right. If they've taken Simon to wherever they've moved this operation, we're going to need help getting him out. And either way, we've not got enough manpower to stop Kingsford."

Darrow nodded. "We need backup and we need it now. If finding Simon leads us to Kingsford, we've got to move fast."

"You think he let us get as close as we did, don't you?" Danny asked.

"Yes, and so do you."

Danny did. He'd known something was wrong, but he'd expected an ambush before they went in. Kingsford obviously wanted them to find out what they did. "They would have pursued us if he'd wanted to keep his secrets and that—"

"Means he's close to his endgame," Darrow finished.

Danny wasn't sure whether to be excited or terrified. He'd worked for five years to put an end to this organization. He wasn't going to fuck that up now.

"I'm calling Nance. It's time she came in on this personally." He pulled out his phone and located the most secret of all the numbers in his contacts.

***

Si woke and fought his way to consciousness. His head throbbed and he could feel something wet and sticky on the back of his neck. Blood, no doubt. He was sitting up, with something hard against his back. A wall? His head had lolled to the side while he'd been unconscious and his neck was so stiff it was difficult to hold his head up. Lights seemed to flash in front of him in time to the pulsing pain. He opened his eyes, squinting even in the dim light of the… cell?

He was in a small room, maybe six by eight, with concrete walls and a single narrow window high in the wall. His arms were pulled behind him. He didn't try to turn his head since that would make him feel even sicker than he already did, but an attempt to move his hands taught him that they were secured to a ring in the floor. How had he ended up here?

He fought the pain in his head. He had to figure this out. Edgar. The last thing he remembered was leaving Edgar. Why had he done that? Where was Edgar now? Oh fuck. The Retreat. They were in the basement and then… what? No matter how hard he tried to tug on the memories, he couldn't remember anything after that. Where were the others? Here— wherever here was—in different cells? Or had they escaped whatever had happened?

He heard keys jingling and then a lock turned. He didn't move or open his eyes, nothing to give away that he was awake.

"Get in there," a gruff male voice said.

Someone groaned and stumbled. They hit the

wall close to him. More rattling. Was someone being chained up with him? The groan hadn't sounded like Danny, Jackson, or Sport.

After what seemed like an eternity, he heard footsteps cross the cell, the door closed, and the lock slid into place again.

Simon waited several more seconds before opening his eyes. "Derrick?"

"Oh thank God you're alive."

"Do I look that bad?"

Derrick smiled. "Yeah."

"Well, so do you."

Derrick nodded and winced.

"What are you doing here? I thought…"

"That I was working for them?"

"Yeah."

Derrick exhaled audibly. "I was."

Anger rushed to Simon's chest, giving him incentive to try to free himself. He yanked on the chains.

"Not because I wanted to," Derrick explained. "They had my family."

"Danny said—"

"The safe house wasn't as safe we were led to believe."

"Oh God, your kids, they—"

"They got out. I was going to join them, but… as you can see, I was caught."

Kingsford was damn good, but Simon was not going to let him win. "So you *were* trying to hint that you were sending me into a trap by giving me more directions than you ever have."

"Yes. I thought you'd get that."

"I did. Then I walked into another trap apparently. Have you got a plan to get us out of here? Do you know where here even is?"

"Did they take you from The Retreat?"

"Yes." Simon was getting dizzy from trying to stay upright. He allowed himself to slump against the wall.

"How long was the trip here?" Derrick asked.

Simon still didn't remember anything that happened after they heard gunfire in the basement. "I don't know. I must have been unconscious."

"Fuck, so was I. My best guess is that we're under Kingsford's main residence in Norfolk."

"So he's hiding in plain sight?"

"Yes."

"Are they listening in or watching us?" Simon asked, looking around the cell for cameras even though the movement made his head feel like it was going to explode.

"I don't know."

They'd have to take the risk. "Keep your voice low and gestures minimal. We need to come up with a plan."

"You think we can get out?"

"I think we have to try. Tell me what you've seen outside the cell."

**

Darrow led everyone to a new hotel. It was far nicer than the last one, but to Edgar, the filthy rooms they'd left would've been paradise if Simon was with him. "What are we doing to find Simon?" he asked once everyone was inside.

Danny started to speak, but Darrow interrupted

him. "I've called some contacts. They're going to let us know when they have intel."

"What contacts? You expect me to accept that?" Edgar was ready to hit someone and he didn't care which of these assholes it was.

"CIA contacts with far better resources than ours."

"You expect me to trust that the CIA isn't in on this shit?"

"Trust Danny," Darrow insisted. "He knows these people and they are our best hope."

Edgar grabbed the keys to his truck, which Sport had laid on the counter. He was done with this. He shouldn't have followed docilely in the first place. "I don't trust fucking anybody right now. If the rest of you want to sit on your asses while Simon is out there, hurt, maybe being tortured, maybe—"

Danny grabbed Edgar's arm to stop him from leaving. Edgar swung around, ready to slug him. Then he saw the fear on Danny's face. He'd tried to tell Simon things weren't as they seemed just like Edgar had. Edgar punched the wall instead.

"Please trust me," Danny begged. His tone scared Edgar. He almost never let his confident mask slip. Edgar's anger dissipated into despair. He turned away on shaking legs, expecting to crumple in on himself. Danny laid a hand on his shoulder.

"Stay with us. We're going to find Simon."

"Fine." But it wasn't fine, nothing was. Simon could be anywhere, and the more time that passed, the lower their chances of finding him. Edgar pulled away from Danny and paced the room.

"Danny told me what you found in Kingsford's

cabin. You all seemed spooked," Darrow said.

"We got shot at and they fucking took Simon. Of course we're fucking spooked!" Jackson looked like he was ready to lose it any second. Edgar was right there with him. "Before we go over that, maybe we should worry about how the hell they knew we were coming and how they managed to hide from our surveillance? What are the chances they aren't listening to us right now?"

Darrow sighed. "I know who the mole is."

Sport watched his boss, his tension obvious even from across the room. "It's bad, isn't it?"

"Yeah, it is," Edgar answered before Darrow could.

"Let me explain before you jump all over me," Darrow said, clearly wishing he didn't have to do this.

"Who the fuck is it?" Jackson asked.

"Reed."

Jackson snarled. "Fuck no. You're wrong about this."

"I wish I were, but he's been lying to us for days."

Jackson moved toward Darrow, but Sport grabbed him, holding him back.

"Explain," Sport demanded.

"He was sending us a dummy feed," Darrow said. "We never saw anything that was actually going on at The Retreat."

"Wait." Sport looked like he was trying desperately to process that and failing. "You're saying Reed deliberately misled us."

"What if he was also misled?" Danny asked.

Darrow shook his head. "He's the one who was in charge of surveillance. Once he knew I'd left my office and that I was taking control of surveillance from the field, he ran."

"Why the fuck should we trust you?" Jackson asked. "Reed was part of my team. He risked his life right beside me. He—"

"I have screenshots of what he sent me and then a few minutes later, men in the woods, waiting for you, vehicles hidden down the road. He told me to send you in. He told me it was safe and that I needed to stop doubting this mission."

"You don't know what he actually saw."

"I know he's gone now."

Jackson ran a hand through his hair and paced the length of the room. "They could have taken him, forced him."

"I have witnesses who saw him leave alone and the equipment he was using has been wiped clean."

"That's why you got Edgar and came after us," Danny said.

"This can't be true. It fucking can't!" Jackson shouted, but there was more pain in his tone than anger now. He sat and dropped his head between his legs. Sport crouched beside him and laid a hand on his back.

"If he's with them, then he fucking let us get ambushed. Dallas's death, that's on him. How? How could he…?"

"Where was he that day?" Darrow asked.

Jackson shook his head. "I can't go back there. I… Don't ask me to."

"I'll tell him," Sport said, the grayness of his face

showing how difficult the memories were for him. "I found Jackson and pulled him out. When I got us to the outskirts of the village, Reed wasn't there. It was just Scott and Tommy. They were slightly banged up but not in need of attention. Reed showed up several minutes later. He looked like someone had beaten the shit out of him. He said they'd captured him but that he gotten free in all the chaos."

"So he fucking staged it," Jackson said. "That fucking bastard let Dallas die and my leg get ruined because some madman promised him what? Money? Power? How the fuck could he do that?"

Sport closed his eyes. "I don't know."

Darrow took a deep breath. "We don't know for certain who he was loyal to at that point. All we know is that he's working for Kingsford now."

"If they were ready for us, why didn't they stop us before we went in? And why the fuck did they let us leave?" Danny asked.

Sport shook his head. "Maybe Kingsford wanted us to know what he was up to. Maybe he's hoping we'll panic and come after him when we're not ready."

"Or maybe he's close to his big reveal and he's taunting us, giving us a teaser of what's to come," Darrow said.

Danny snarled. "Nothing is going to come because we are going to find him and tear him apart."

"What if he wanted Simon for some reason? What if this was all about him, something Kingsford wants from him, something he thinks Simon knows?" Edgar asked.

"Whatever the hell his game is, they must have

been watching us down in that basement," Danny said. "They timed the attack perfectly. I was just about to start photographing the documents when they started firing. Now we've got no proof, nothing but our word."

"What did you find?" Darrow asked.

Edgar looked around the room. Danny looked sick. Jackson was still fighting memories and Sport looked close to panic, which, based on what Simon had told him, was very unusual. Edgar wondered if any of them were going to be fit for the next step in this fucked-up mission. But fit or not, he would never leave Simon at the mercy of those bastards. Simon could walk away from him a thousand times, betray every declaration of love they'd shared, and Edgar would still go after him, because no one deserved to be left in hell.

"We need a plan," Edgar said. "We can't just sit on our asses."

"We've got to wait until our sources get back to us," Danny said.

"You really think we can trust these people? Some shadowy sons of bitches that you won't even name for us?" Edgar asked.

"I seriously doubt I know any of their real names and if I did, I'm sure as hell not authorized to reveal them, but yes, we can trust them."

That wasn't good enough for Edgar. "You know as well as I do that the chances of us finding Simon alive decrease with every delay. We need to go in now."

"You think the five of us can really handle this without support?" Darrow asked. "If we charge in and get killed, where does that leave Simon?"

Edgar lost it then. He charged Darrow and pinned him to the wall. "This is the man I love and I'm fucking going after him no matter what you say. You got that?"

"What I understood is that you don't give a damn about the odds. Rather than sit still for—"

"Fuck odds. I'm not letting Simon sit there any—"

Sport tried to intervene. "Don't do this." He pulled Edgar off Darrow. "Darrow's a good man. He just wants us to—"

"Sit here on our asses when he won't even tell us who the fuck we're waiting on or why."

Edgar shoved Darrow against the wall once more. Then he walked away. He knew he was being unfair. Darrow was handling things the way he saw fit. They needed someone with a little more distance to make a decision, but waiting was fucking killing him.

Danny moved in front of Edgar. When he looked up, the wariness in Danny's eyes put him on guard.

"I put a tracker in Simon's phone. The kind we can turn on even if the phone is off."

"And you didn't bother to fucking tell me this until now?" Edgar's anger exploded again. He punched Danny in the face, sending him reeling.

Sport pushed himself between them, but Danny didn't make a move to defend himself. He just righted himself and rubbed his jaw. "Damn, you have kept yourself in shape. I guess I deserved that, but I didn't tell you because I didn't want to get your hopes up in case it didn't work."

Edgar nodded because he understood and yet he itched to hit someone else. He'd punch them all if it would help anything, but it wouldn't. "That's what we're waiting on? His location?"

"And backup," Darrow added.

Jackson stood and joined them. "If Reed was working for Kingsford, are we sure he's the only one, or could someone else be tattling on us?"

Darrow frowned. "Derrick's disappeared."

"Fuck!" Danny shouted. "I really wanted him to be on our side."

"He may have run to avoid being pulled in farther, but we don't know and we can't trust him."

"What about his family?"

Darrow glanced at Edgar, and Edgar actually felt sorry for the man. "They're missing too," Edgar said. "The safe house was compromised."

"Wait, you knew that and didn't tell me?"

Edgar held up his hands. "You want to hit me now? Go ahead."

Danny shook his head. "No."

"Derrick is a friend. I get it. Darrow told me when we were on our way to The Retreat."

"So do we think Kingsford's it?" Sport asked. "Or are there other players still? It doesn't seem like he'd be running this on his own."

"I'm sure he's not," Danny said. "But we haven't found anyone else as high-ranking as Kingsford, Arthurs, and Zenk."

"So we get Simon, take out Kingsford, and then regroup?" Jackson asked.

"Yes," Darrow said.

"I'm all for that," Jackson said. "But like Edgar,

I'm not inclined to trust a bunch of unknown spooks."

"Danny, what do you think?" Sport asked. Danny looked more pale and worn than Edgar had seen him since their captivity in South America.

Danny laughed, but the sound was bitter. "I understand Jackson's concern, especially considering that Reed betrayed us, but we can't do this alone, not fast enough anyway. We'll have to trust our instincts."

"Like with Reed?" Jackson said with disgust.

"He was on our team," Sport said. "We had every reason to assume he was loyal just based on that."

Jackson shook his head. "I should have known."

"No, don't do that to yourself." Danny's phone interrupted him before he could say more. He glanced down. "I don't recognize the number."

"It could be Nance," Darrow said.

Edgar scowled. "Now we get a name?"

"Hello," Danny said. "Oh thank fuck." He looked up at everyone. "They found the signal. We know where Simon is."

CHAPTER NINETEEN

Yes. Fuck, yes. We're getting out of here. Simon had found a rough spot on the wall, and though he practically had to dislocate his shoulder to pull himself far enough up to rub the rope binding his wrists on it, he'd frayed it enough that he could just pull his hands free.

"Derrick?" Simon's former handler had been in and out of consciousness since he'd arrived. He wasn't sure Derrick could hold it together to escape, but he wasn't going to leave him there.

Derrick stirred. "Someone coming?"

"Not yet, but when they do, I need you to be ready."

Derrick opened his eyes and shifted to look at Simon. "It worked?"

Simon was reassured that Derrick remembered the plan. He'd seemed rather out of it when Simon had explained what he wanted to do. "Don't move until I tell you to and then do exactly what I say."

"Okay," Derrick mouthed. God, he looked bad. *Please let this work.*

Time seemed to creep by, but eventually Simon heard footsteps, someone coming to the cell, hopefully a low-level lackey bringing food, someone Simon could overpower with little effort.

The lock turned. The door opened, Simon readied

himself. Reed Devereaux stepped in.

Simon exhaled and dropped the ropes, no longer needing to pretend he was restrained. "Thank God. How'd you find us?"

"No," Derrick said at the same time. "He's not—"

The punch seemed to come out of nowhere. Simon's head slammed into the wall and he blinked, trying to right himself. Reed spun him around and fastened cuffs on him. "I told them ropes would never hold you. I don't know what the fuck they were thinking. At least I got here in time."

"You're the fucking mole?" Simon wasn't sure he'd said the words out loud. He wasn't even sure he was conscious.

Reed laughed. "I'd actually thought you might figure it out, but evidently you're as gullible as the others."

Simon kicked out, catching Reed on the shin. All that earned him was a shove that made him lose his balance. His head was ringing and he could hardly see straight. If he hadn't been concussed before, he sure as hell was now.

How had he been so stupid? He knew better than to trust anyone and yet he'd thought the world had thrown him a lifeline. Fuck, he was a fool. And now... He needed Edgar and he might never see him again.

He struggled as Reed secured the cuffs to the ringbolt that had held him before. Spots danced in front of his eyes, and he was sure his head was going to explode at any moment. He had no chance to overtake a man nearly as strong as Simon at his best.

"Where's everyone else? Did you let them walk away?" Had he really seen his friends rushing into the woods as Kingsford's men had dragged him to a vehicle, or was that part of a dream?

"We let them go. They'll come for you and your traitorous friend," Reed said. He kicked Derrick, and the crunch sounded like one of his ribs breaking.

"You fucking bastard. You're the traitor, not Derrick. And my friends have no idea where I am."

"Don't worry. They'll find you. Never leave a man behind and all that bullshit."

Simon wished Reed had been left behind, left to die in the jungle or on a sinking ship. He deserved that and worse. "What did Kingsford offer you?" Simon was stalling, trying to figure out a way to escape, but there was no way in hell he could walk, much less fight his way out.

"Power, strength, the chance to actually effect change instead of just taking orders. Instead of going on mission after mission and never really accomplishing anything, being hampered by rules and protocol, I could actually be the weapon I was meant to be."

The sick son of a bitch. "And fucking over your friends didn't bother you?"

"So you're Mr. Morality all of a sudden?"

If only Simon could face him at full strength. He'd tear the bastard apart. "No, but I don't betray the people I care about."

"Are you sure? What would Edgar say about that right now?"

Those words hurt more than being thrown against the wall, more than if Reed had stabbed him in the heart. Despite being barely conscious, Simon yanked at his chains, desperate to hurt Reed.

Reed shook his head. "You're pathetic right now, but you do have spirit. You might get lucky. Kingsford might still be willing to let you work with him, at least after he has a little fun with you."

Still? Reed's words jolted Simon like an electric shock. Suddenly he was back there in the "clinic" he'd been taken to after the attack on the *Ridgeway*. His arms chained to the bed. Edgar gone. There was a man in the doorway, watching him. Kingsford.

Fuck! The men there, they'd been with him. What had Kingsford said to him then? The harder he tried to remember, the faster the image faded.

"I will never work for that goddamn son of a goatfucker no matter what he does to me!" Shouting used the last of his strength. Simon slumped against the wall, barely conscious. His limbs felt like weights.

"It will be fun to watch you change your mind." Reed left, banging the door shut, the sound rattling Simon's brains.

"I'm sorry," Simon mouthed to Derrick as Derrick's face faded and darkness swallowed him up.

***

Admiral Kingsford's base was at his own fucking house. Edgar couldn't believe the bold bastard was hiding this shit in his fucking primary residence in Norfolk. But now they knew and they were going to end it all. Victoria Nance, head of whatever nonexistent branch of the CIA Danny and Simon did or did not work for, was coordinating the strike. Edgar had spent the last few hours pacing the hotel suite, listening to her argue with Jackson—who didn't take orders well, not that any of them really did—and reminding them both that he didn't give a fuck what they thought was priority, he was there to get Simon fucking free.

Maybe he'd gone a little insane. The operation had to be shut down. Kingsford needed to pay. He'd ruined countless lives, and from what they'd learned it sounded like he was getting more psycho by the day. But no way in hell was Edgar going to go anywhere but straight to where they thought Kingsford was holding prisoners and guinea pigs for his fucking experiments—possibly they were one and the same. If he touched Simon, if he—

"Edgar, are you sure you should be here?" Danny asked. He glanced at Sport. The three of them were stuck waiting in a van parked across the street from Kingsford's house.

Edgar read the question on Danny's face as if he'd spoken out loud. "If you think I'm going to wait in the car like a—"

"Can you be objective?" Danny asked.

"Can you?"

Danny leaned away, the sting in Edgar's tone strong enough to pierce even his thick skin. Years of chasing this man, trying to find all the players, not knowing who was on your side and who wasn't. Danny was as fucked-up as Simon and no way in hell was he ob-fucking-jective.

"This is my world," Danny said. "You chose to get out."

Fuck, no. Edgar was not having this fight now.

Sport laid a hand on Danny's thigh. "If it were me in there, would you sit in the van?"

Demonic anger flashed in Danny's eyes. "Fuck no. I'd burn the place to the ground."

"I'm going in there and I'm getting Simon," Edgar declared. "And then I'm going to marry that son of a bitch, tie him to the bed, and never let him go."

"Good plan," Sport said.

Danny's eyes widened. "What does that—?"

The radio chirped, interrupting them.

"Everyone's in place. Get ready to go in on my signal," Nance said. She had a strike team in place to take out the perimeter guards after her pet geek—as Danny referred to him—took out the security cameras.

"We're ready," Danny responded.

Fuck yes, they were. It was all Edgar could do to keep still. He watched on the surveillance monitor in the van. Without zooming in, they could see the gaudy monstrosity from the street. At least the fucker owned a lot of property well outside town. They wouldn't have to worry about neighbors and their safety.

***

Simon heard gunfire and shouting. Was it in his head? Was it real? He opened his eyes. He was on his side on a concrete floor, his arms twisted behind him.

"Are you awake?"

Was that a real voice?

"Simon? Something's happening out there."

"Derrick?"

"Yes, do you remember where you are?"

Simon's closed his eyes. His thoughts wouldn't come together. "Edgar."

Silvia Violet

"No, he's not here, unless he's with whoever is fighting out there."

Fighting. Edgar. "Kingsford."

"That's right. We're in a cell… somewhere, and yeah, Kingsford's responsible."

Simon tried to sit up, but a wave of nausea had him lying back down before he vomited. "I'm fucked."

"Yeah, you took a fucking hard hit to the head. I'm glad you're awake."

"Reed? Was that a dream?"

"No, he's working for Kingsford and he threw you against the wall. You probably already had a concussion before that."

"Fuck." No wonder he was so messed up.

"Yeah."

"So what's happening?"

"I wish I knew, but try to stay awake. We might have a chance to get out of here." Derrick held up his hands; he wasn't chained like Simon.

"How?"

"I might have fractured my wrist, but I managed to slip them off."

Damn. Derrick was more badass than he'd thought. "I should try that."

Derrick shook his head. "No, just stay awake, I'm going to see if I can look out the window. Derrick attempted to find holds in the concrete block wall, but he didn't have any luck.

"Someone's coming," Simon warned.

Derrick froze. "I don't hear anything."

Did Simon? Or was his brain tricking him? No, someone was coming. "Trust me."

Derrick moved back to where he had been restrained.

Footsteps jogged along the corridor. Gunshots. Three. Then the footsteps again. Simon tried again to sit up. He managed to lever himself up using the wall as support. His stomach still threatened to revolt, so he stayed as still as he could and took slow breaths. He had to be ready if someone came in. He was not going to die without seeing Edgar again. Derrick tensed, ready to attack.

The tiny window in the door slid open and a face appeared.

"Edgar?" Simon asked.

"Simon. Thank God." Keys rattled. The lock turned and Edgar stepped into the room.

"Tell me you're not with Kingsford," Derrick said, standing and letting Edgar see that he was free.

"He's not," Simon declared before Edgar could answer.

"Reed is," Derrick said.

"We know."

You didn't tell me? Simon wasn't sure if he voiced the words or not.

Edgar bent and unlocked the chains on Simon's ankles and his wrists. Simon tried to stand and that was more than his body could take. At least he managed to turn from Edgar before he wretched up bile. How long had it been since he'd eaten?

"How bad off is he?" Edgar asked Derrick.

"He already had a head injury and then Reed threw him into the wall—Simon didn't know he couldn't be trusted. He was out for hours. He woke when the shooting started."

"How are you?" Edgar asked.

"Better than Simon. Better than I was yesterday."

"We've got to get out of here. Come on, Si. I'll carry you."

Simon turned. Were there two of Edgar? That didn't make sense. He swayed, but before he could fall, Edgar caught him and lifted him into his arms.

Derrick said something, but Simon couldn't make out the words. Edgar tossed Derrick the keys and he went one way while Edgar turned the other.

"Derrick?" he mumbled.

"He's looking for other prisoners."

Others. Couldn't leave others behind. "Should help."

"You can't even walk. I'm getting you out of here."

Simon held on as Edgar moved quickly through the hall. He fought the nausea and the darkness that wanted to pull him under.

Edgar stopped and Simon opened his eyes. They were in a different part of the... house? "Where are we?"

"Kingsford's house, but there are two men blocking our exit. I need to put you down so I can deal with that."

"His house?"

"Yeah, in Norfolk. You were in the basement."

"Fuck me." Derrick had been right. Was it Derrick who'd told him where they were?

"Later. I promise."

Simon smiled though Edgar couldn't see him. His head swirled as Edgar lowered him to the floor. He looked up, then squeezed his eyes shut as a light from a window threatened to blind him. "This is the best I can do. Don't move. I'll be right back."

"No, I—"

Edgar bent and looked right into Simon's eyes. *Fuck, he's gorgeous.* "You stay here. Let me take care of this."

You're always taking care of me. His voice still wasn't working properly.

Edgar moved silently, keeping himself pressed against the wall. Simon wanted to stop him. He was the one who should be taking care of Edgar, not the other way around. Edgar waited at the corner and then disappeared.

Simon jumped when a shot echoed down the hall.

Seconds later, a gun slid along the floor stopping about five feet from Simon. *Get it.* He shifted position and the world tilted. He ended up facedown on the floor.

Someone was coming from the other direction. From the sounds of fists making contact with flesh, Edgar was still fighting with the men around the corner. Another shot and then a body landed on the floor. Edgar appeared around the corner, locked in combat with a man. Who had taken the shot?

The footsteps were getting closer. *Get the fucking gun.*

This time Simon managed it. He had to crawl, but he did it. A man appeared wearing body armor. He aimed at Edgar, who had his back turned. "No!" Simon lifted the pistol and shot him through the head. *Fuck yeah. Perfect aim even when I'm half dead.*

"Simon?"

Danny's voice. Was it real? Was any of it real?

"He fucking shot him," Danny said. "He fucking saved you."

"Simon?" Edgar now. "Simon, are you with me?"

He tried to nod, but the world faded.

***

Edgar carried Simon. He was unconscious now. Danny covered them as they made their way to the back entrance. Things seemed quiet outside, but shouts came from all over the house.

Danny pulled out his radio. "We're at the back door. Edgar has Simon. He needs a medevac."

"Roger that. Send them to the gate. We've almost got this wrapped up."

"No sign of Kingsford?" Danny asked.

"No."

"Fuck."

Edgar had hoped one of the other teams had captured or killed him. "No one's found Kingsford?"

"No, and I doubt he's here anymore. Take care of Simon and then we'll regroup."

Edgar held Simon in a way that stabilized him as much as he could. He hated how exposed the stretch of lawn was, but they had to get out of there. He moved quickly, but he didn't run, not wanting to jostle Simon any more than he had to. He saw two of Nance's men at the gate. When he was within feet of them, one raised his rifle and took a shot. He heard a shout behind him, but he didn't turn around. *Keep walking.* He saw Nance and several men clustered around an SUV.

He felt like he was moving in slow motion, but finally he made it.

Before he could say a word, he and Simon were surrounded by CIA medics. "I'm a doctor. I can do this," he insisted, but Darrow pulled him away. "Let them handle this. You're hurt too."

Edgar looked down at his leg. A bullet had grazed him, but he'd ignored it. Blood had soaked his pants and they clung to him, dark and sticky. "I'm fine." He brushed Darrow off, but he stumbled when he tried to take a step. "Dizzy."

Darrow took his arm and lowered him to the ground. "It's a miracle you haven't passed out already. What the fuck was Danny thinking sending you out alone like this?"

"Wasn't alone. I had Simon. Didn't even feel it." Now he did, though. Looking at the injury seemed to have made it real.

"They're going to check you out and then you can examine Simon and tell them everything they did wrong."

Edgar flipped Darrow off. "He needs to go to a hospital."

"And so do you. You can ride together."

"No, I'm—"

Nance stepped into Edgar's line of sight. "No arguments. Darrow will go with you. We're making a last check to clear the house and then there's nothing here but cleanup."

"Kingsford?"

"No sign of him."

"Jackson and Sport?" Edgar asked as he let his head hang between his legs. He was not going to fucking faint. He was a fucking doctor, for Christ's sake.

"They checked in a few minutes ago. They're following a lead on Kingsford."

"Reed."

"Jackson found him. He won't be bothering us anymore."

Edgar shivered, imagining the retribution Jackson had exacted. His vision started to go fuzzy.

"Make him lie down, for fuck's sake," Nance said.

Darrow took his arm and then the world went black.

CHAPTER TWENTY

Edgar had been sitting by Simon's hospital bed for hours, waiting for him to wake up. The only amusement he'd allowed himself was texting with Laura and letting her try to cheer him up with a series of god-awful puns.

When Derrick had filled him in on the hours Simon had been a captive, Edgar couldn't believe Simon had fought so hard to get free despite his injuries. But his complex concussion had finally taken its toll. By the time Edgar had gotten him out of Kingsford's house, Simon had been severely dehydrated. He was covered in numerous cuts and bruises, but nothing other than the head injury worried the doctors. For once, he hadn't even needed stitches. Edgar's leg ached and every time his pants rubbed the wound it stung, but it wasn't serious and he'd refused to do anything but sit by Simon's bed once he'd been treated.

Now it was a waiting game. He should have woken up by now. When Simon had collapsed after saving Edgar, Edgar had been terrified. But Simon had been thoroughly examined at the hospital—it had been torture to turn Simon over to other doctors even if Nance insisted they were the best—and the doctors expected him to wake up whole and ready to fight his way out of his hospital bed. Simon never stayed in a medical facility willingly, but after almost twenty-four hours, he was still out. With every hour that passed, Edgar worried more that there was damage no one was seeing.

"Fucking head injuries," he muttered.

"What?"

Edgar's heart skipped a beat. "Simon? Oh my God, you're awake?"

Simon blinked and looked around. "Am I? I'm not dreaming?"

"No," Edgar said. *Please let him be okay.*

Simon tried to reach for him, but his IV hampered him. Edgar reached out and took his hand. "You're really here?" Simon asked.

"Yes, do you know where you are?"

Simon looked around a little more. "Fucking hospital. Looks like."

"It is. What do you remember?"

Simon closed his eyes and took a deep, raspy breath. Edgar handed him a cup of water, smiling as he remembered Simon's earlier demand for a bendy straw. Now he had one.

"Kingsford. His house? Is that where I was?"

Edgar nodded.

"You saved me," Simon declared.

"I found you, but you saved my life when—"

"Some bastard was going to shoot you in the back."

Edgar smiled, thrilled that Simon remembered what had happened before he lost consciousness.

"Are you okay?"

"Now that you're awake, yes." He squeezed Simon's hand and was reassured even more when

Simon squeezed back. "I should let your doctor know you're awake."

Simon frowned. "You're my doctor."

His words sent warmth through Edgar. "Always, but I don't have privileges here and... I was a little banged up myself."

Simon grinned. "I bet you pitched a fit about that."

Edgar remembered how he'd grilled Dr. Wilson when she'd come to talk to him about Simon. "A little."

"I don't want another doctor."

"I know and I'll be here, but..."

"Go ahead. Let's get this over with so I can get out of here." Simon sighed dramatically, which told Edgar he was his old self.

"You're not leaving before—"

"Don't argue. Just call the doctor." Yes, Simon was definitely going to be fine.

***

Edgar stepped into Simon's room late the next evening, reassured by Dr. Wilson's report. Simon was looking out the window, a troubled expression on his face. "Are you okay?"

"I left you."

"Not really, but you've been asleep for a while."

Simon frowned. "No, before I was in that cell. I left you. You wanted to come with me."

"Oh yeah. You did."

"Why aren't you angry?" Simon looked unsettled. This was not the time to go into Edgar's sentiments on being left behind. Just thinking about Simon walking away after cuffing Edgar to the fucking bed made Edgar's hands clench into fists. He hadn't forgotten even if he had forgiven. "Trust me. I'm pissed as hell and as soon as you're better, I'm going to take it out on your ass."

Simon's eyes widened. "You are?"

"Yes, you're lucky you were captured actually."

Simon raised his brows. "Am I now?"

"Yes, because if you'd come out of The Retreat with the others, I would've beaten the shit out of you."

Simon scrunched up his face like he was thinking hard. "Nope. I would've preferred your fists to theirs."

Edgar brushed Simon's hair off his face. "You scared me."

"I know. I'm sorry. That sounds so fucking lame. Can we get back to how you're going to punish me?" Simon licked his lips.

"You can't possibly be horny now."

"Oh, but I can. You're here. That's all it takes."

Edgar's cock reacted to Simon's words. Knowing that after the hell of the last few days, Simon still felt that way made him wish Simon was healed and they were somewhere else.

"It's so boring lying here. I'm sure you can think of something that will amuse me."

Edgar did not need this temptation. "Simon, this is not happening."

"You're the one who brought it up."

Edgar couldn't deny that. "I was provoked."

"At least kiss me. You haven't kissed me properly since I woke up." Edgar realized what was really happening. Simon might be bored and horny, but more than that he was scared, scared something wasn't like it used to be, that Edgar was backing away from him.

"I kissed you when you were sleeping."

"Well, that's fucking creepy." Simon smiled as he said it, though. He liked the attention. Edgar was sure of it.

"Hmm. If I'm a creep, then maybe I shouldn't kiss you now."

Simon narrowed his eyes. "You fucking better."

Edgar smiled. He braced himself on either side of Simon, determined to be gentle with him.

"I still won't break," Simon protested. "Even in here."

"I'm not taking any chances." Edgar kissed him, gently at first, just the lightest pressure against his lips. Simon brought the arm that wasn't tethered to an IV pole around Edgar's back and tried to pull him closer, but Edgar resisted. "Relax, let me do this my way."

Simon started to protest, but Edgar stopped him by deepening the kiss. Simon opened for him, welcoming Edgar's tender exploration of his mouth. He took it slowly and kept his weight off Simon, but the longer the kiss went on, the more he wanted to devour him. He licked at the roof of his mouth, his lips, his jaw, and then his throat.

"More, Edgar. I need more."

Simon had been stuck there two days, though he'd spent most of one unconscious. Knowing Simon, that was longer than he ever went without jacking off, which he couldn't properly do with an IV in his right hand. Edgar brushed his fingers carefully down

Simon's body. Si hissed when Edgar brushed the top of his cock, which was hard and reaching for him.

You cannot fuck him here in the hospital. But maybe…

He slid his hand lower, rasping the top of his palm over the sheet, just barely giving Simon friction on his cock. Simon arched up. "Dammit, don't tease me."

This was fucking crazy. "How long do you think it's been since a nurse came by?"

Simon made a face like he was concentrating. "Not long, plenty of time for fucking."

"Simon McLeod, you are not getting fucked until you're fully recovered from your concussion."

"You sure about that? Because if you won't, I can always look elsewhere."

Edgar snarled and leaned down close to Simon like he might kiss him again. Instead, he said, "Don't even think about it. You're mine and if anybody fucks your obnoxious little ass, it's going to be me."

Simon sucked in his breath. "Fuck, you keep talking like that and I'm going to come all over these sheets with no other provocation."

Goddammit, Edgar loved the effect he had on Simon. He pulled the sheets down until he could grab the edge of Simon's hospital gown and lift it.

"See," Simon said. "If they hadn't meant for you to fuck in a hospital, why would they make it so easy?"

Edgar didn't bother responding to that. He raised Simon's gown enough to free his cock. Simon groaned as Edgar stroked him slowly. He heard something in the hall and froze.

"Don't stop, please," Simon begged. "Anyone comes in, I'll just send them away."

Edgar chuckled, imagining Simon telling a nurse that he was busy and she had to come back later. He'd never been an exhibitionist and he hoped no one walked in on them, but he didn't really care if they did. He slid his hand up Simon's cock and watched a bead of precum form in the slit. Before he even realized what he was doing, he bent and licked it off.

"Holy fuck! Please tell me you're going to—"

Edgar took Simon's cock into his mouth, cutting off his question. He worked Simon with his mouth, sucking, licking, nipping. He'd only intended to tease him, but once he'd gotten a taste, he couldn't stop. This was only the second blow job he'd given in his life, and his lover was in a hospital bed with a concussion.

Simon whimpered and whined and muttered "don't stop" over and over. Edgar couldn't have even if half the hospital staff had walked in. It was going to be a miracle if he could keep from coming in his pants.

***

Simon shuddered as Edgar took his cock deeper than he had before. The heat of his mouth was making Simon insane. He'd never thought Edgar would do this, suck him off right there in his fucking hospital bed. He'd thought he might get a hand job, but this… Thank God he wasn't on a heart monitor anymore. It would be going crazy.

He couldn't take his eyes off Edgar. He was so fucking hot with his lips stretched around Simon's cock. Simon wanted it to last forever, but it had been so long since that day at the seedy-ass hotel when Edgar had fucked him on the bathroom counter, fucked him until he couldn't see straight.

"Oh fuck!" Edgar took him deeper and Simon couldn't help but shout. "So fucking good, so—" Edgar swallowed around him and that was it. He was right there on the edge. "Edgar!" He tugged on Edgar's hair, but he didn't move.

Simon couldn't hold back anymore. He arched up, pushing his cock deeper into Edgar's mouth and letting go of him so he could bite down on his hand. If he let out the shout building in him, he'd summon every nurse on the floor.

Edgar hung on, swallowing over and over. When he finally pulled off, cum dripped down his chin, Simon's cock jerked once more in response to the sexy sight. "Fuck."

"Yeah." Edgar licked his lips and then stood.

"Where are you—?"

"Just getting something to clean us up."

Edgar entered the bathroom and came back a few seconds later, all traces of Simon wiped from his face. He cleaned Simon up as much as he could and tucked him back in. "Thank you," Simon said.

"No problem. I didn't want you to have to get out of bed."

"I mean for…"

Edgar cupped his chin and forced him to look into Edgar's eyes. "That was for me as much as for you. There's no need for thanks."

Warmth radiated through Simon's chest. Edgar still loved him. "Really?"

"Yes."

A loud knock sounded on the door and then it swung open to reveal a woman with long straight blonde hair wearing a business suit that likely cost her thousands.

"Simon's still not ready to talk to anyone yet."

The woman gave an indelicate snort that didn't fit with her polished appearance. "If he's ready to fuck, he's ready for questioning. At least I had the courtesy to wait until you'd finished."

Simon watched an adorable blush creep up Edgar's neck. "You heard us?"

She laughed, the sounds somehow more chilling than merry. "I think the whole floor heard you."

Simon didn't know the woman, but something about her voice was familiar. "Who the hell are you?"

"Victoria Nance." The woman extended a hand. "I keep forgetting we've never met in person."

"Fucking hell. I thought you were a myth, something created to give new agents nightmares."

She smiled and Simon could see the ruthless fighter in her. "I occasionally take corporeal form."

"Agent Nance orchestrated the attack on Kingsford's house," Edgar explained. "After Danny told her what you'd found."

"I thought you didn't do fieldwork," Simon said.

"We couldn't wait once we knew what Kingsford was up to. The op needed an expert and I'm the best, so I came in."

Simon grinned. That sure sounded like Nance. "But Kingsford got away."

"So you were awake to hear that?" Edgar asked.

Simon nodded. "Yes, unless I dreamed it."

"I wish it had been a dream, but the fucking

bastard escaped. We're going to find him, though. He's lost most of his supporters and access to his funds. He won't get far." She looked at Edgar. "You can leave. I have classified questions for Simon, but I promise not to damage him much. I'll leave that to you."

Edgar's face turned even redder. He was so goddamn cute. "Simon's recovering from a serious head injury. Whatever you have to say—"

"Can't wait."

Edgar was not going to win an argument with this woman. "It's okay, Edgar. Let me talk to her. Then you can help me get out of here."

"You are not ready to go home. Just because you're—"

"Fine. Whatever, just come back in an hour, okay?"

Edgar glared at Nance. "Do not tire him out."

She smiled, but there was nothing soothing in her expression. "I'm quite sure Mr. McLeod can handle what I have to say. He's not a fragile flower."

"No, but he's mine." Edgar closed the door.

Simon whistled. Not many people got the last word with Nance.

"I like him," she said. "I hope you plan to keep him."

Simon smiled. "Oh, I definitely do."

CHAPTER TWENTY-ONE

Edgar hadn't seen Simon in over two weeks, and now the bastard wasn't even responding to texts or calls. He'd understood that Simon needed to spend some time at Langley. He had a shit-ton of debriefing to do along with making plans for the future, plans that might or might not include him getting the fuck out of the life he'd been immersed in for years. Kingsford was still out there and Edgar knew Simon wouldn't rest until he was found, but he hoped Simon would at least consider other options afterward. Edgar wouldn't leave him, though, whatever he chose. Simon was his and that wasn't going to change no matter whether he was a CIA agent or not.

The doorbell rang, interrupting Edgar's thoughts. Who the hell was bothering him now? He wasn't in the mood for a visitor, not even Laura. They'd hung out a lot since he'd returned home. She'd been sympathetic and encouraging, but he wasn't in the mood to be comforted. He was more in the mood to beat the shit out of someone—so much for the mild-mannered doctor façade. Maybe he'd take a long punishing run once he got rid of whoever was at the door.

When he looked through the peephole, his breath caught. Simon was standing there. He looked so much better than he had in the hospital. His color was back and the only visible sign of what he'd been through was a gash on his forehead that hadn't completely healed.

Edgar turned the lock and yanked the door open. He gave Simon a quick once-over. "At least you didn't show up unannounced because you'd been shot, stabbed, thrown off a bridge, or mauled by wild beasts."

"Hey, that last one never happened. Well, never when I had to show up here."

Edgar snorted and Simon moved past him into the living room. "You could have at least answered one of my texts today."

"I was driving. And I wanted to surprise you." Simon kicked off his shoes and started unfastening his pants.

"I thought you'd taken off on some fucking mission without even telling me. I was ready to drive to Langley and fuck somebody up."

"How about you fuck me up instead?" Simon ripped off his T-shirt and tossed it on the floor.

Edgar deliberately ignored him, not sure whether to be annoyed or flattered than Simon couldn't seem to get naked fast enough. "I have questions, you know. I suppose you'd have told me if Kingsford had been found."

"Fuck yes, I'd tell you no matter who told me not to."

Damn right. "And Derrick? How is he?"

"He's fine. He's with his family at an undisclosed location." Simon's pants hit the floor, leaving him in nothing but socks and boxers.

"Okay and what about Nance? Has she—"

"Can we debrief later? I feel like that's all I do lately." Simon, now completely naked, wrapped a hand around his cock and stroked.

Edgar feigned annoyance. "Is sex all you think about?"

Simon stroked faster. "It's been weeks. I need you."

"Phone sex didn't work for you?"

"It was like an appetizer. I need the full seven-course meal."

"Seven, huh?"

"At least. Now get over here." Simon backed up until he was next to the foot of the bed.

Time to put him out of his misery. Edgar stalked toward him and Simon's hand moved faster as he did. Edgar unfastened his own jeans. He shoved them and his boxers down his legs and stepped out of them, glad he hadn't been wearing shoes or socks.

He pulled his T-shirt over his head and tossed it on the floor, letting Simon see how much he wanted him without needing to say anything. Simon studied Edgar's body as he brushed his thumb over the head of his cock. When his eyes met Edgar's, he licked his lips.

"You want a taste?" Edgar asked.

"So fucking much."

Edgar raised his brows as if to say *then take it*. Simon let go of his cock and stepped closer. He leaned in and ran his tongue along Edgar's neck as he caressed Edgar's torso. Then he grasped Edgar's hips, anchoring himself as he pinched one of Edgar's nipples while drawing the other into his mouth. "Fuck. That's… Fuck!"

Simon laughed, his breath warm against Edgar's sensitized skin. He moved his kisses lower, dropping to his knees. Edgar fought to stay still, to let Simon enjoy himself, when he really wanted to throw him on the bed and fuck him until he begged for mercy.

Simon licked at the thin skin over Edgar's hipbone, then buried his face in the dark hair surrounding his cock. "I love how you smell," he murmured.

"Si."

He looked up, eyes bright and too blue to be real. "What?"

Edgar's cock was so hard he didn't think he could stand it any longer if Simon didn't do something about it. "You've got five seconds to start sucking my dick or I'm turning you over and driving it into your ass."

"So it's a win-win situation for me?"

Edgar thrust his hands into Simon's hair and tugged his mouth toward the tip of Edgar's cock.

Simon didn't resist, not that Edgar had thought he would. He tongued Edgar's slit and pleasure sizzled along his limbs. Simon smiled as he continued to tease, licking, kissing, even tugging the tight skin of the shaft with his teeth.

"Five. Four. Three."

Simon gave him a dazzling smile and then slowly ran his tongue up the underside.

"Two. One!"

Simon swallowed him down, taking him all the way to the back of his throat. Edgar gasped. "Fucking fuck. How do you do that?"

Simon pulled, dragging his lips along Edgar's

cock, eyes closed, a look of pure ecstasy on his face. He sucked and licked Edgar's cock until Edgar was thrusting against him, desperate for more. Just when Edgar was certain—as much as he'd been determined to shoot off in Simon's ass—that there was no turning back, Simon tightened his grip on the base of Edgar's cock and pulled off him.

***

Simon grinned as he patted the edge of the bed and then the side of Edgar's thigh. "Leg up here." He'd had this planned for a long time. He doubted Edgar had ever had anyone's tongue in his ass, and Simon was eager as fuck to be his first.

"What? Why?" Edgar still seemed to be processing that Simon had actually stopped him from coming.

"You'll see. And you'll thank me."

Edgar narrowed his eyes, but he did what Simon asked. Simon rewarded him by lavishing attention on his balls, drawing each one into his mouth and rolling it around. Edgar squeezed Simon's shoulders, holding himself up.

It's only going to get worse, baby. Simon moved his focus to Edgar's perineum, licking and giving him pressure with his tongue while he circled Edgar's hole with a finger. Then he shifted position so he could reach farther back.

When he flicked his tongue over Edgar's entrance, Edgar jerked. "Fuck, Simon."

"Relax, you're going to love this." Simon teased him, flicking the opening with the tip of his tongue, licking as he pulled Edgar's ass cheeks apart to give himself better access.

"Oh my fucking God, Simon."

Simon laughed. Then he speared Edgar, forcing his way past tight muscle, opening him up with his tongue.

"Simon!"

He ignored Edgar's strangled plea and tongue-fucked him until he was putty in Simon's hands. Edgar was working his cock so fast his hand was a blur. Simon sucked two of his fingers until they were dripping with spit. Then Simon pushed Edgar's hand away and took Edgar's cock back into his mouth as he pushed a finger into his ass. Edgar gasped and squeezed Simon's shoulders hard enough to bruise. Simon pulled off his cock long enough to say, "Don't hold back."

Edgar didn't. He fucked Simon's mouth while Simon added a second finger and drove deep to find his prostate. When Simon pressed against that sweet spot, Edgar shuddered. "Fucking fuck!"

Simon did it again and Edgar cried out. "Too much. Too fucking much."

Simon worked him, driving his fingers in and out in the same rhythm Edgar was using to thrust against his face. When he was sure Edgar was on the edge, he brushed over his prostate again. Edgar stiffened, shouting Simon's name as he came.

***

When the lightning storm that had lit him up subsided, Edgar crawled onto the bed and collapsed. He'd heard about the joys of prostate stimulation, but holy fucking shit he hadn't thought it could be that good. And the feel of Simon's tongue in him. That had been the hottest thing ever!

Simon flopped onto the bed next to him. "Liked that, did you?"

"Why the fuck hadn't we done that before?"

Simon laughed. "I have no idea." Edgar reached out and ran a finger along Simon's cock, which was deeply pink and dripping precum onto his stomach. Simon gasped, but he pushed Edgar's hand away. "You liked having something in your ass, didn't you?"

"More than I thought possible."

Simon gave him a wicked grin. "So do you think you might want to try…" He looked at his straining cock suggestively.

Edgar realized he did. If Simon's fingers felt that good—stretching but not hurting—could his cock feel good too? "Yes. Definitely, yes."

"Turn over."

Edgar got to his hands and knees, heart still thumping wildly from his orgasm. This just might do him in, but he needed to know how it felt for Simon to fuck him. "So you like it both ways, top and bottom?"

"Oh yes, and I'm going to make sure you do too. Where's the lube?"

Edgar reached out and snagged the handle on the nightstand drawer. He grabbed the bottle of lube and tossed it toward Simon.

When Simon pushed a slick finger into him, he couldn't hold back a groan. As hot as it had been to have Simon's fingers inside him, Simon's cock was a lot bigger. "It's going to hurt, isn't it?"

"It's going to burn at first, but then it's going to be heaven. Trust me?"

Silvia Violet

"Okay." He was too curious not to.

Simon got into position behind him and rubbed the tip of his cock over Edgar's ass. "You've got to relax," he said, leaning over Edgar and taking Edgar's cock in his hand. Simon stroked him until he was driving into Simon's fist. Then Simon pushed against his ass, opening him up.

Oh fuck! Edgar felt like he was being split in two.

"Relax, breathe, and push against me."

"How am I supposed to relax when you're about to fucking impale me?"

"Remember how good it felt when I hit your prostate?"

He did. "Yeah."

"This is going to be better." Simon surged forward as he said that and Edgar pushed out. "That's it. Open up for me."

Edgar's ass burned and Simon's cock simultaneously felt wrong and yet so fucking right. "More." He wanted it all. The pain was a like a tease, not like any pain he'd felt before, but like his body knew it was a prelude to pleasure.

Simon pulled out and Edgar gasped. "That feels fucking amazing."

Back in again, deeper this time. "You're going to fucking break me."

"No, not yet anyway, not until I'm really fucking you."

"This isn't really fucking?"

Simon laughed as he pushed deeper. This time he didn't stop until Edgar felt his balls slap against Edgar's ass.

"All the way in," Simon said, the satisfaction in

235

his voice making Edgar want to flip him off, but his arms were shaking too much for him to risk lifting one.

Simon laid a hand over Edgar's tailbone, his fingers caressing Edgar's sweat-slick skin. "You okay?"

Edgar took a deep breath. "Yeah, I am." He was as stuffed as a Thanksgiving turkey, but something about that feeling was just fucking perfect. He shifted on his hands and knees, unable to stay still.

"You ready to really be fucked now?"

Edgar nodded. "Show me what you've got."

Simon leaned over him and put his mouth close to Edgar's ear. "You shouldn't have said that."

Before Edgar could reply, Simon pulled out and then drove back in. Edgar gasped, pain and pleasure mixed, and he thrust back, taking Simon even deeper. Simon established a fast rhythm, and Edgar didn't have time to think or to do anything but hold on. Then Simon shifted position slightly, and his cock slid over Edgar's prostate. "Fuck!"

"Good, huh?"

"Don't ever fucking stop."

Simon's cock didn't hit that sweet spot every stroke, but when it did, Edgar jerked, feeling as if someone had just lit up his cock with pure pleasure. "Close, so fucking close," he said, reaching for his cock. He had to have friction, had to have more. "Harder, Simon. I'm not going to fucking break."

"Hey, that's my line. You can't steal it."

Edgar's witty comeback fled from his mind when Simon drove in harder than he had before. Then he did it again and again. Edgar stroked himself faster.

The next time Simon slid over his prostate, Edgar cried out, saying God knows what, possibly he was speaking in tongues. All he knew was that he'd never come so hard in his life.

Simon followed him, driving against him and losing his rhythm as he pumped against Edgar's hips. Edgar felt the hot flood of cum in his ass. "So fucking hot," he muttered into the pillow.

When Simon pulled out, Edgar winced. "Fuck, I think you broke me after all."

"Then I did my job right," Simon said. He leaned over the side of the bed and grabbed Edgar's T-shirt. He wiped himself off and then tossed it to Edgar. "I do have towels, you know," Edgar said.

"You've also got a washing machine."

Edgar was too tired to protest. He cleaned himself and then threw the shirt on the floor.

"Stay right there," Simon told him. He slid from the bed and stumbled toward the living room.

Edgar glared at him. *He wouldn't get out of bed to get a towel a second ago. What's so important now?*

When Simon returned, he was carrying a small box.

"Come here." He motioned for Edgar to move to the edge of the bed.

"What the hell are you up to?"

Simon didn't answer. Instead, he got down on one knee.

"Si?"

"Edgar, will you marry me?"

Edgar stared at him wide-eyed. He hadn't been joking when he'd thrown out a proposal weeks ago, but he'd been afraid to bring it up again, despite his declaration the day they rescued Simon.

"Showing up unannounced wasn't my only surprise." Simon opened the box, showing Edgar two matching gold bands. "If you don't like them or if—"

"Yes," Edgar said, grinning at his future husband.

Simon looked down at the rings. "Are you sure?"

"More than I've been about anything. I meant it when I said you were mine."

Simon ran a finger over one of the rings. "I want to wear it now, but we should wait until we have a ceremony."

Edgar nodded. Simon put the box on the nightstand and climbed onto the bed. Edgar pulled him into his arms, spooning him. He could tell Simon needed reassurance. "I would have asked you again eventually."

"Yeah?"

"Yeah."

They didn't need any other words. They'd declared their love with their bodies, and now, they'd made a promise to declare it to the world.

***

Simon woke up sometime later that afternoon. He was still pressed against Edgar with Edgar's arm draped over him. He'd have been happy to stay right there forever if his damn bladder wasn't threatening to explode. Too much soda on the drive there.

Edgar was awake when he returned, sitting up propped against the headboard. "When do you have to go back?" he asked.

"Not until tomorrow. They tried to tell me I

couldn't leave yet, but I told them I had something very important to do and they'd be damn lucky if I came back at all."

Edgar held out his arms and Simon settled on the bed between his legs and leaned back against his chest. "It's okay," Edgar said. "I know you have to finish this."

"Things have gotten even more complicated."

"That's possible?" Edgar asked.

"Yeah, we've hit these bastards hard but Kingsford's still out there and he's still got supporters. I'm not supposed to tell you this, but Kingsford was with me."

Edgar ran his hands up and down Simon's arms as if trying to soothe him. "At his house?"

"No, in the clinic after the *Ridgeway*, after they took you away."

Edgar sucked in his breath. "And you never told me?"

"I didn't know. My memories of that time are hazy and they come and go, but when Reed was in the cell—"

"You mean when he was beating you, a man he'd worked with. A man who was already injured."

Simon sighed. "Yeah. He said there would *still* be a chance I could join Kingsford and that brought back a partial memory."

"So those fuckers who sent me back to the States were working for him. Does that mean you were working for him for a time?"

Simon closed his eyes and breathed deeply. "Maybe. Derrick wasn't being controlled by him when I was first assigned to him, though, only for the last six months or so. I always knew there was a chance all my missions had different objectives than were stated to me outright. Apparently Kingsford offered me a chance at 'greatness' if I would work for him. I didn't respond well, but for some reason he's still interested in me. I've got to find out why."

Edgar nodded. "Yeah, you do."

"And I need to ferret out who at the CIA is still helping him."

"And then…"

Simon was hesitant to let himself hope that one day this would truly all be over. But they were close, weren't they? Close to the end? "Something different. I've had enough danger and enough time away from you."

"If danger's what you need, if an operative is truly who you are, then I'm not going to force you to leave. I want you to do this for yourself, not because I told you to."

Edgar's acceptance made Simon love him even more. "I have something else to live for now. You."

"Lie down on your back," Edgar insisted. Simon's heart pounded as he did so. Edgar straddled him and pinned his arms above his head. Simon couldn't help the quick intake of breath as Edgar molded their bodies together. "I love you," Edgar said, but Simon didn't need the words. He could see it on Edgar's face. "I love you when you're risking your life and when you're lying here in bed, and whatever comes next, I'm going to love you through that too."

"Because you're mine," Simon said.

Edgar raised a brow and leaned close to Simon, almost close enough to kiss him. "That goes both ways." He kissed Simon then and Simon arched up into him, suddenly as needy as if they hadn't just fucked each other like wild beasts. Edgar drew back from the kiss and Simon raised his head, chasing Edgar's lips, not wanting to stop.

"I love you," Edgar said. "I don't want to wait until this is over to get married."

"Wait? Who said anything about waiting? I'd marry you right now."

Edgar looked down pointedly. "We should probably get dressed first."

"No getting dressed until you fuck me," Simon protested.

"Fuck. Shower. Clothes. Marriage license. How does that sound?"

"Perfect." Simon had never been happier than in that moment. He was there with the man he loved and they had a future that involved more than dodging bullets. "Can we get a house and a dog and all that shit cozy married people have?"

Edgar laughed and rolled them until Simon was on top. "We can get anything you want."

"Oh yes, we certainly can." Edgar kissed Simon then and neither of them said anything else for a long time.

Dear Reader,

Thank you for purchasing *Unexpected Engagement*. I hope you enjoyed it. If so, make sure you've read the first two books in the series, *Unexpected Rescue* and *Unexpected Trust*. If you like gay romance with suspense elements, you may also enjoy the *Fitting In* series. The first book is titled *Fitting In*. I offer a free book to anyone who joins my mailing list. To learn more, go to http://silviaviolet.com/newsletter.

Please consider leaving a review where you purchased this ebook or on Goodreads. Reviews and word-of-mouth recommendations are vital to independent authors.

I love hearing from readers. You can email me at silviaviolet@gmail.com. To read excerpts from all of my titles, visit my website: http://silviaviolet.com/books.

Silvia Violet

Author Bio

Silvia Violet writes erotic romance in a variety of genres including paranormal, contemporary, and historical. She can be found haunting coffee shops looking for the darkest, strongest cup of coffee she can find. Once equipped with the needed fuel, she can happily sit for hours pounding away at her laptop. Silvia typically leaves home disguised as a suburban stay-at-home-mom, and other coffee shop patrons tend to ask her hilarious questions like "Do you write children's books?" She loves watching the looks on their faces when they learn what she's actually up to. When not writing, Silvia enjoys baking sinfully delicious treats, exploring new styles of cooking, and reading to her incorrigible offspring.

Website: http://silviaviolet.com

Facebook: http://facebook.com/silvia.violet

Twitter: http://twitter.com/Silvia_Violet

Pinterest: http://www.pinterest.com/silviaviolet/

Tumblr: http://silviaviolet.tumblr.com/

Titles by Silvia Violet

Coming Clean
If Wishes Were Horses
Needing A Little Christmas
One Kiss

Fitting In
Fitting In
Sorting Out
Burning Up

Unexpected
Unexpected Rescue
Unexpected Trust
Unexpected Engagement

Wild R Farm
Finding Release
Arresting Love
Embracing Need
Taming Tristan
Willing Hands
Shifting Hearts
Wild R Christmas

Galactic Betrayal
Abandoned
Deceived

Available from Dreamspinner Press
Denying Yourself
Pressure Points

Available from Changeling Press
Savage Wolf
Sex on the Hoof
Paws on Me
Hoofin' it to the Altar

Available from Loose Id
Astronomical
Meteor Strike

44494846R00138

Made in the USA
Middletown, DE
08 June 2017